THE KILTON GIRLS

THE KILTON GIRLS

LEXIE LEE ELLIOTT

carrowmore.ie

Main Characters

Emily O'Hara, the daughter of Erin and John O'Hara, who are Catholic farmers in Kilton.

Her friends are Siobhan McGrath, Ellen Monahan, Charlotte Hogan and Sarah Beaver.

Noel Howard, son of Bertie and Miriam Howard, who are Protestant farmers in Kilton.

His friends are Jack, Tom, and Terence.

Bernard and Madge Byrne, are owners of Byrne's grocery and hardware store, and the post office within the store.

Bronwyn Redmond is the local nurse, and very involved in the parish.

Beatrice Ruth, an aristocrat and widow of the late husband Freddy Dunbar, lives in Kilton.

Lorraine Mulrennan, the parish librarian; her sister Elizabeth, brother-in-law Paddy Reynolds and their son Mike, are farmers in the parish.

Johnny and Rose, owners of Mythen's public house.

Aiden Rath, bank manager, his wife Claire and their son Terence.

Oliver Nugent, farmer in the parish, loved by almost everybody and full of his own importance.

Acknowledgements

I would like to give a special thanks to Ronan and his team at Carrowmore Publishing for making this possible, for all his patience, which has been very much appreciated.

A heartfelt thanks to everyone who helped me make this book possible: to my husband Patrick and family for all the support you all gave me; to Anne Marie O'Connor for all your invaluable help, for Diana Ryan, Sinead Hudson and Amanda Thomas for all the fun we had on the Mondays when I was writing this book, I miss you girls.

My mother Alice Howard Dunbar a storyteller herself.

For Fiona Kiernan, thank you for all your encouragement and Patricia Murphy, author, thank you for your advice.

For my late friend Elisabeth (Betty) Kiernan who encouraged me to finish this book, I miss all the stories and the endless cups of coffee.

CHAPTER ONE

The End of College Years

Emily's father, John, collected the young friends from their digs in the heart of the city and proceeded to make his way home. The girls were giddy with excitement at the sight of Kilton. Home at last and their first stop was Madge's shop. Madge, a well-built fine-looking woman, stood still for a moment, just to look at the four young friends.

She called out for Bernard, ordering John to take over the shop just for a few minutes. She was pleased to see the girls, and they were glad to see her. She was, after all, their second mother and wanted to catch up on all the gossip.

Madge brewed up a pot of tea, and as luck would have it, she had made a chocolate cake for her friend Bronwyn's birthday the previous night and there was plenty left over.

After an hour or so, the girls made for home, John dropping each one of them off at their own house.

When they had gone, Bernard, a tall man with broad shoulders and a head of dark curly hair, thought happily about how highly the young girls thought of Madge, and how happy they had made her.

The Love Match

It was the next Saturday night when Noel laid eyes on Emily for the first time. Well, he had seen her before in the local shop, and out on the tennis court when she was a young girl, but that seemed a long time ago now.

This time it was different. She had developed into a beautiful young woman and he couldn't take his eyes off her.

Emily, Ellen, Charlotte and Siobhan planned to go to the local dance on Saturday night. The girls had waited a long time for this weekend. It wasn't only about the dance, it was about pushing those heavy sacks of books off their backs after years of studying. It was time for some fun. They hadn't a care in the whole world, for now, at least.

The girls made their way up to the mineral counter for a choice of orange juice or tea and to catch up with some old friends. Emily was aware that someone was looking at her though. She could feel it, and as she turned around slowly, she caught Noel looking over. He turned away as fast as he could.

He was embarrassed to be caught, but he just couldn't resist. After a couple of minutes, he was caught again.

Emily was having a good look herself, but came back to earth quite quickly when she heard Charlotte calling her to one side with a quiet whisper.

'Don't even think of it Emily O'Hara! He is not for you. A big 'No'. He's a Protestant!'

'Well now, Charlotte, I am not planning on getting married just yet! After the years I spent in college, my parents would kill me. Plus, I want a bit of fun first!'

Siobhan and Ellen looked on with concern, and Charlotte started to giggle. 'Such commotion over nothing.'

The girls decided to go back over to the seating area and wait to be asked up to dance. It was something they weren't comfortable with. After all they were educated woman, and were not about to settle for any man who thought that the 'little woman' should be delighted and honoured to be asked.

It was settled that the girls just wouldn't get up to dance with a fella if they did not want to and would let the men down as gently as possible. And of course, they would never insult a fella, making them feel small, that is unless it was that little weed Mattie Mack, with those bloody x-ray eyes, as he looked right through you. Any girl would run a mile if they saw him coming in their direction to ask them up for a dance. He would send shivers down your bones.

Emily felt a ripple of excitement run through her whole body as she looked back over at Noel. Maybe she had imagined it. Was there some kind of connection between them? She'd never experienced this before.

At that very moment, her friends Charlotte and Ellen caught a hold of her and made their way over to the ladies' room.

'This is just to cool you down!' they screamed with laughter as they splashed water on her face.

Siobhan straggled behind the girls, carrying the handbags, her pink silk embroidered scarf trailing behind her on the dirty sticky floor.

'That should do the trick, Em,' they laughed.

'Did you see that look on his face?' said Emily. 'I think he is a fine fella that's all.' Her friends weren't too sure if that was all.

It was time for a cup of tea and some of Alice Molton's lovely fruit cake, Alice was a very popular woman in the parish. The girls went to the tea counter. Everyone was in fine form. The girls and the men were hanging out over at the counter. Noel made his way over for the tea. He found himself standing beside Emily and Charlotte. He was feeling awkward at being so close to the girls. He could have kicked himself for being tongue-tied. He wished with all his heart he could be like his friend Jack, a charmer who got the girls all the time. Whenever he tried to go over to Emily, he froze. He was sorry he didn't get a chance to introduce himself to her properly before she left the dance to go home.

The first stop on the way home was Emily's house.

'Come on in,' she insisted.

'Do you not think we drank enough tea for one night?' quipped Ellen. They entered the large homely kitchen, an aroma of freshly-baked tarts spreading throughout the house.

The four women sat down and began to tell Mrs O'Hara all about the goings-on at the dance, as they demolished a large tart between them, with a pot of tea. Of course, no one mentioned Noel Howard, but plenty was said about that sleazy Mattie who couldn't keep his hands off any girl. Yes, there were some loose women at the dance who weren't a bit fussy. 'No morals at all', they told Erin O'Hara. Charlotte added to the conversation, that some of those women had standards and wouldn't put up with the likes of him, and pushed him away using very colourful language.

Time raced on, as it always does in good company, and it was soon time to go.

'We must go before Mrs O'Hara starts making breakfast, girls,' Ellen piped up.

The girls bid the O'Haras goodnight and drove the rest of the journey home before the early morning light shone through.

This summer was to be a fun time for the girls. Ellen drove her Morris Minor everywhere. The local hard-working lads in the village garage made sure Ellen's car was well-oiled and running well. The men were very fond of Ellen. She was a lady, a decent girl, who they wouldn't dream of overcharging. They wanted to help her, not rob her, and always had a conscience where Ellen was concerned. Of course, not everyone got the same treatment!

Emily made her way upstairs, deep in thought. Her mother observed her pretty young daughter. She knew the girls hadn't told her everything about the dance and wondered what her daughter wasn't telling her. Emily felt elated and tired at the same time. 'Bloody hell, he's so handsome and seems a real gentleman,' she thought. She couldn't help but notice those deep blue eyes. She also noticed his white, straight teeth and how they brightened his whole face when he smiled. Every time she thought of him she felt a lurch in her stomach. The only way she could describe these feelings was that it was like being on a boat on a turbulent sea. She wondered if it could be love. She had never felt anything like this before.

She couldn't forget that look in his face. Then it dawned on her. For crying out loud! she thought. She hadn't even talked to him let alone kissed him. 'Get a hold of yourself Emily Anne O'Hara,' she told herself, 'you are being foolish.' It was time to move on with her life. A match like this simply wouldn't or couldn't be tolerated. Or could it?

CHAPTER TWO

A Woman You Can Trust

'Janie mac, girls, said Siobhan, 'we simply must talk to Madge about Emily. She sure is lovesick for that Noel chap up on the Howard farm. She hasn't bothered to look at any young men at all!'

Although she had many invitations to go to one thing or another, she was showing no interest whatsoever.

It was a beautiful summers day in early June and the year was 1952. Ellen left her car behind. The girls decided to ride their bikes down to the village to buy some ice-cream, but of course they had much more than ice-cream on their mind. The girls went down to Madge's shop, where you could tell her that you murdered someone and where you'd buried the body, and not even the priest would get it out of her. Madge got all the gossip of what was happening around the parish, and beyond. She knew what everybody was up to. Of course, some people would put their own slant on things, but this time Ellen, Siobhan and Charlotte had a mission in mind and needed Madge's trusted help.

Madge loved to see the girls calling: Charlotte Hogan with her head of red curls, loads of freckles and those inquisitive hazel eyes, Emily O'Hara with those piercing blue eyes and her long wavy blonde hair, Siobhan Mc Grath, with hair like a raven, black and as smooth as silk, with those beautiful big green eyes, and Ellen Monahan with her olive skin, dark brown hair and brown eyes, that looked like they were about to pop right out of her head, when in deep conversation about a topic that mattered to her.

The Glue that Keeps Everything in Place

'Bernard, Bernard! Are you going deaf or what?' said Madge. 'Will you take over for fifteen minutes or so? You can see the girls have dropped in. We're off to have a cup of tea.'

Madge made her way in to the kitchen with a madeira cake tucked under her arm. Bernard, her long-suffering husband is only too happy to oblige.

'Make sure you find out where the body is buried!' he laughed, as the girls disappeared into the kitchen. 'We could do with a bit of extra money. Isn't that what you call blackmail?'

He liked to see his wife solving people's problems. She was at her best when she was in the thick of it. He always thought Madge had missed her true calling. He had not doubt that she would have made a good counsellor.

He wished with all his heart they had been blessed with children, though neither of them blamed the other. They both always had felt it had been God's will. Bernard had an empty feeling like there was something missing inside him. He couldn't make out what it was. He had a very full and busy life. He loved his wife and she loved him. They ran a good business together and got on with just about everybody in the parish, that is except for those two biddies, Maggie and Peggy, and of course some other undesirables who usually kept him on his toes. His life was busy, all right. 'You would need eyes in the back of your head,' he complained to his wife. It was needed to run this business well.

Ellen spoke to Madge about Emily and how she was in love with Noel Howard.

'She can't seem to get him out of her mind. But we think she is totally out of her mind. She shouldn't want to settle down yet. She still has a lot of living to do. What do you think, Madge?' said Ellen. 'Do you think you could find anything out from Noel's mother when she's in doing her shopping, like if he's seeing anyone?' Ellen continued. 'Please don't make it obvious that we are talking about Emily!'

Charlotte piped up in a more serious tone,

'It might be embarrassing for Emily if Noel's mother picked up on it and Noel found out Emily liked him so much.'

All four girls had graduated from college earlier in the week. After leaving their digs, they exchanged addresses, and promised to keep in touch with the many friends they had made during their time in Dublin. They were excited and sad at the same time to be leaving their college years behind them. It was time to contribute to society. Were they ready? Emily and Charlotte had secured jobs in the local primary school, while Ellen was to teach teenagers in the convent school.

Then there was Siobhan, the odd one out. She dressed so very well and always managed to turn heads with her beautiful clothes. She was a very glamorous young lady in every way. She had studied at the College of Art and Design. The girls knew they could trust her judgement on any purchase when buying clothes. She had an eye for fashion and style, matching classy pieces with the fashion of the day. She knew how to mix and match colours, that's for sure. She would say what suited someone and what looked like 'a dog's dinner', a favourite saying of hers. Anyone that knew her never took offence at how she told it as it was. They might be wounded for a moment and then they usually got on with it. Her advice was taken on board and the girls learned from it.

Siobhan bought her very first sewing machine at the age of fifteen. Throughout her younger years her mother would tell her friends,

'Sure, she has every pillow slip in the house cut up for her dolls. I must watch every piece of spare material I have in the house. Of course, I can't complain. I'm happy for her, at least she won't go naked with a God-given gift like that.'

Not much had changed since then except that she had grown up and bought her own material to make beautiful dresses.

Her eighteenth birthday had been a special occasion. Siobhan, her mother and her friend Emily set off to Dublin to buy some material for the occasion: a roll of pale-yellow silk with some deep-yellow velvet trimmings for the sleeves and the neckline of the dress. It was always an easy task for Siobhan. She had magic hands when it came to making beautiful clothes, her friends would say, wishing they had that special gift.

'I suppose it is like singing. You either have it or you haven't,' Emily remarked to Charlotte.'

Ellen was a gentle young woman, who moved slowly, meaning she didn't jump into anything hastily. She put a lot of thought into everything she did. Her taste in fashion was quite different from her friends. She liked smart tweed costumes, and had a collection of cream and white blouses, with some finely knit jumpers. She wore court shoes, and the odd kitten heel shoe. Ellen wore her hair clipped back off her face when working, and had a selection of coloured hair slides, matching her attire for each working day. Well, the nuns had been delighted with Ellen, she always looked so neat and pretty. It was agreed by all that she also had a personality to match.

Ellen's first choice when choosing a career was teaching. Nothing else would do. She loved going to college to study for secondary school teaching. She knew in her heart that she would do the very best for her students and that she genuinely wanted to make a difference in their lives. Primary school teaching did not appeal to her at all, as she felt there was nothing quite like the inquisitive mind of young teenagers.

Unfortunately, not every student was interested in studying. For some people, it was more like putting in time until a match was made in the farming community between their sons and daughters. Of course, they weren't the only ones to look for a good match for their children.

Una was one girl who caused an awful lot of trouble in school. She had the nuns and lay teachers worn out from the time she came to school in the morning to last class in the evening. All she did all day was doodle on her books and she simply refused to do any study. Mother Mary was left shaken at what she had witnessed. Una forgot her lunch, and wanted to go home at lunchtime. Mother Mary wouldn't hear of it and told her not to worry and that no one died of hunger in a couple of hours. She would have a sandwich made up for her in the convent kitchen in any case. Mother Veronica brought it out for the young girl. Una walked over to the bin and shouted at the poor nun.

'If you think I am going to eat your fucking bread and margarine, you have another thing coming! Do you hear me? You lousy bitch,' she said then added some more appalling language as she fired the sandwich in the rubbish bin.

Una's parents were sent for and told that this kind of behaviour would not be tolerated in school. At the same time, they asked her parents if her home life was just as troublesome and if there was an explanation as to why was she so unhappy. She would have to show respect to the teachers if she was to remain in the school. The nuns decided to give Una another chance, asking Ellen would she be willing to work with this troubled child. The young teacher took on the challenge.

Emily had looked forward to going to college. She wanted so much to become a primary school teacher. She had a love for children and was immediately drawn to any shy child who stood back, almost hiding behind their mother. Emily read beautiful stories for the young children, which always stirred up their imaginations. Lorraine, the local librarian, never minded giving over a little space for these inquisitive youngsters for an hour on a Saturday morning. It wasn't always easy to get the youngsters beyond the library door, and Lorraine was always very glad of whatever help she could get from these educated women of the parish. 'Books were always a good investment for any child,' said Lorraine to the mothers, encouraging them to have some in their home.

Emily had a strong personality and was a born leader. If she had a disagreement with someone, she would let them know she was annoyed. She was always able to stand her ground and didn't suffer fools gladly. She was a boss and everyone would have to toe the line, if she was in charge of the jumble sale or a sale of works. Everything had to be done to her specific instructions. 'Miss Bossy Pants', people would call her, but that didn't bother her at all. She had a thick skin. If a job had to be done, she was the one to see that it was done properly. She had a mind of her own. If she set out on a mission she rarely ever failed.

At times Emily behaved like a tomboy. But her sense of style told a different story. Amongst her clothes, she had a collection of pleated satin dresses with drop waists, pearls, gold chains and bracelets, which were all the rage in the roaring twenties. Her friend, Siobhan, would run them up in jig time on her machine. Emily was definitely unique. No one else had her style. She loved all colours, but her favourites were blue, green and cream. She had a fair collection of soft woollen cardigans, satin and silk wraps, her handbags were made of leather and satin, and a collection of kitten-heel shoes in cream, black and brown. She had a wardrobe to die for, the girls told her every time they wanted to borrow a piece of clothing for some occasion.

Charlotte was always in a hurry, racing up and down stairs, trying to fix the world. She had an opinion on everything and was always trying to make things better for the less well-off in the parish. She sought the help of people who gladly gave their time in doing up the local hall, which was in a bad way. The smell of must and damp hit you the minute the door was opened. There was wallpaper peeling down from the walls. The wine-coloured paint had well faded and the stairs were not safe to walk up. A lot of work was needed to put the old hall back in some sort of order. Raffle tickets were sold all over the parish, bringing in much-needed money. First on her list was to set up a committee to to run the hall. A games room, table tennis and badminton were her main priority. Tea and Marietta biscuits were a bonus for the evenings when the hall was open.

Johnny Mythen was a jolly, small, slim man, with hair receding back from his forehead. His wife Rose had a head of blonde curly hair and pale blue eyes. They ran one of the local public houses in the village and had placed money boxes on their counter for the parish hall, alongside Blessed Martin and Saint Anthony boxes. Some of the local people, when doing their shopping or having a drink in their local pub, might throw in a couple of shillings or coppers, whatever they could afford for the upkeep of the hall. Nearly everybody in the Parish had children, who would all benefit from it. The hall was for everyone's use, all were welcome except trouble makers. Madge heard all the gossip in her shop, so she would always give some advice if there were problems, not that it would be taken by some of the committee members.

'I don't mean Charlotte now!' Madge said to her husband Bernard and her friend Bronwyn.

In her college years, students loved being in Charlotte's company. They knew if one needed a job done, she was the one to get it sorted.

'A real suffragette if there ever was one,' said Madge. 'And now, she is pushing the women of the parish out of their comfort zones, making it a better place to rear their children. She would do well, in helping women's rights to move forward and in making a difference in their own country.'

Bronwyn agreed with Madge, saying, 'No doormat need apply. Only strong women to make the world a better place.'

Charlotte was unquestionably tough but had a great charm about her. People gravitated to her. But of course, not all. Noel was a tall lean man, with blue eyes and blond hair. He had made up his mind the moment he set eyes on Emily, deciding that he was going to marry this girl. He had no doubt in his mind that she was the one. He just knew.

The Best of Friends

Noel's friend Jack had caught him looking over at Emily. He knew that look. He himself had that same longing in his eyes when he first laid eyes on Gina, but it was never going to happen for them. She had been visiting the neighbourhood, had spent at least seven weeks in the parish with some relatives, and both had spent the best part of a summer in each other's company. Those lovely warm days had stretched out before them and everything had been perfect. They spent a lot of time together and she had left a lasting impression on him. He had lost his heart to this girl. Such pain he felt when she went back to America! It took him a long time to get over her. He heard later that she married an American. Obviously, she didn't feel the same way about him. It just wasn't meant to be. It took him a long time to shake off the feelings he had for this girl.

Noel had been a good friend throughout this hard time in Jack's life.

'My friend, this simply wouldn't work, not at all. Mixed marriages seldom work. You can't get involved with their kind of people. They are a good decent family, not short of a couple of bob in the O'Hara household. A marriage like this would bring its own problems. Martha Power's father is a Church of Ireland minister!' he continued. 'She is a pretty enough girl. Not much money but the right faith. So how about it Noel?'

He thought his friend Jack had lost the plot altogether. Noel thought him a right eejit. He had no intentions of getting married! Well, not just yet.

Noel, Jack and the rest of the gang made their way home, each going their separate ways. Noel's mother and father were still up. They were always relieved when Noel arrived home safe, though they would never let him know they were worried about him. He was home early enough. In a few hours, he would be working out on the farm. His father was smoking his old rosewood pipe whilst doing the books and his mother was about to put away the iron, her last pillow-slip left neatly on top of the pile of ironing and to have a well-earned cup of tea before bed. His mother called out to Noel, telling him she had just made a fresh pot of tea and to give it a minute or two on the hob.

The minute his father Bertie saw him he knew he had something on his mind and it had nothing to do with the farm.

'What happened at the dance tonight, son? How did you all get on?'

'We had a good old night and met up with some of the local lads, and of course there is always a stranger or two, the usual lot of rowdy vagabonds who are there to cause trouble. You know the crowd I'm talking about?'

Next morning over the eleven o'clock mug of tea, Noel carried on the conversation from the night before.

'Oh, I forgot to say there was a few good-looking women at the dance.'

His mother glanced at her son from under her glasses as she was putting the finishing touches on a jumper she was knitting for her hardworking husband.

'You mean girls,' she said with a broad smile.

Both parents had never seen their son moonstruck before.

'Yep, that is exactly what that look is,' said Noel's father to his wife. 'Ah, I remember it well Miriam,' he smiled, then gave his wife a big hug. 'Let's hope it will pass, and if not we can only hope she will be the right girl.'

Noel spent the next couple of weeks working hard on the farm but every morning when he woke up, this blue-eyed girl kept coming in to his head. 'Feck's sake,' he thought, 'I have to do something. But what?' Why was he taking so long to make the move in her direction? Was it the faith thing, as in, like they say, that she is not one of us? What trouble would be brought upon the two of them? How presumptuous of him, he thought. He hadn't met the girl since the dance a good while back. He hadn't even kissed her. Did she feel the same way about him? He could almost feel it, a connection between them. He couldn't possibly be mistaken, or could he? Was he just another love-struck young man? These feelings will pass with time, Jack kept telling him.

A couple of months had passed, but he still felt the same. He wasn't at all interested in taking any other girl out. This girl had stolen his heart completely. He could still see Emily in that lovely blue satin dress, the way she wore her hair, right down to her lovely silver shoes. It was funny how he remembered every little detail about her. Noel decided to go for it!

Over Sunday dinner Noel couldn't keep still because he was so nervous. His father asked him what was the matter and if he was alright. Noel announced to his parents that he was in love with Emily for quite some time but that he had never made any kind of contact with her. He told them how he felt this relationship wouldn't be tolerated on either side, and he presumed this courtship would be difficult, even impossible. It would be upsetting for them both, he told them, and that it was what held him back for so long and the reason he had taken a while in making up his mind.

It took his parents a while for it all to sink in. They had seen a want in him for a long time, but couldn't quite put their finger on what it was. At least now they understood why he was never interested in bringing a girl home. It was obvious now there was only one girl for him.

But of course, Noel's parents weren't at all pleased with their son's choice! She might be a nice girl but not one of them. With a heavy heart his father spoke to his son.

'Well now you know in your heart,' he said, 'that is why you held off so long. This just won't be possible, son. Not possible at all!'

A Time for Change

As time went on Noel worked harder every day, putting in all the hours God sent. He would never go against his parents' wishes, for now at least. His father thought that it was about time for Noel to take a break and visit some of the family beyond Dublin, and work on their farm for a couple of months.

'He might just see a little more of life for a while, maybe go to some dances and outings and see how he gets on,' Noel's father, Bertie, said to his wife Miriam. 'Maybe he'll put all this nonsense behind him'.

His wife thought it seemed like a good idea and was in total agreement with her husband.

'We can get help from my brother Dan,' Bertie went on. 'He might let one of his strong sons up from the farm in Kerry for a couple of days to help bring in the harvest. They probably could do with a bit of a change too.' They were a family of all boys. 'I know they won't mind once I explain the situation and there are plenty of big lads down there. I am sure they can spare one of the boys.'

Jack came to see Noel off. His pal wouldn't be around for at least three months. Jack wished his friend the best and teased Noel about keeping the home fires burning, meaning taking care of the girls in the parish, while he was away. Not that Noel was too interested in any of them anyway! Jack placed his hand on his friend's shoulder. They were like brothers as well as good friends and they knew as the train pulled out of the station that they would always be there for each other, no matter what.

Summer Days

'Why don't we book a game of tennis for Saturday afternoon girls?' Ellen said to Emily, Siobhan, and Charlotte.'

'I know you are not a bit interested in the sport, Charlotte. You prefer your stuffy old books,' Emily said, making fun of her friend.

'Ah, that's not fair,' said Charlotte pleading her case. 'I just can't see the sense in chasing a silly ball around a cement court. Or on grass for that matter. Why not ask Sarah and see if she can make it? I hear she is quite good at tennis. At least she will give you a decent game,' she continued. 'I will sit on the benches and have some water for all of you when you need it. Who knows, maybe I will meet the man of my dreams as I sit looking pretty, while all of you are suffering from exhaustion with all that perspiration rolling down your face! Hmm, Charlotte,' she said talking to herself now, 'that sounds like it has possibilities!'

Would fate come into play, she thought or would it simply be luck, if she were to meet that someone special?

'We are far too young to settle down!' Emily said to her friends. 'We need to look forward to our new jobs. What an exciting time it is going to be for all of us! It's not such a good idea to be looking for a husband yet.'

'Who said anything about a husband and settling down?' Charlotte spoke up. 'Before you know it we could find ourselves walking up the aisle. Are you all mad? That is not going to happen for a long time?'

The four friends make a gesture, putting out their hands each one on top of the other, giving a look of fierce independence to one and other.

A Time to Reflect

Noel enjoyed his time working on his uncle's farm, the dances, bringing in the harvest and all the banter with the hired help. Although he did worry about his father not having enough help on his own farm! But his father had told his son on more than one occasion when talking to him on the telephone that he had plenty of help with his young cousin up from Kerry and he of all people should know about all the good neighbours who help one another to bring in the harvest.

'It's a time when everyone is equal on this grand land of ours, and one's religion does not come in to it at all,' Noel's father said to his wife. 'Only good company, a bit of fun as well as plenty of hard work. It's a good neighbourly time when everybody enjoys each other's company with a good heart and plenty of grub.'

The girls were in fine form as they rode their bikes on a lovely sunny afternoon on their way home from one of their many trips to Madge's shop, after having tea and some of her gorgeous coffee cake. They bumped into Emily who was coming in the opposite direction. She had been helping on the farm and hadn't a minute to spare. She had just left her house to go down to Madge's to post some letters for her mum who had a sister in America. Every time Emily's mother wrote to her sister, it was the same story. Each time she tried to read the letter back it was almost impossible with all the tear stains on the paper, she missed her sister so much. It was always such a painful task for her mother to put pen to paper. Emily would buy her mum her favourite bar of chocolate and give her a hug, to take the edge off the loneliness she felt for her sister so far away.

Now or Never

Emily got a puncture on her bike. The girls were trying to fix it when, just in time, Noel came up the road in his green jeep, which ground to a halt. He jumped out.

'What have we got here girls?' he said. 'Give me that bike and I will see if I can fix it!'

Emily's mouth went dry. She froze on the spot and was hardly able to speak. It was mended in a jiffy. Noel knew it was good luck to run in to the love of his life. He felt his heart take a few leaps. It was now or never, he thought, as he tried to fight off the nerves.

'Miss O'Hara, would you be interested in coming to the picture house with me on Friday night?' said he, addressing Emily with a broad smile. He could hardly take it if she turned him down. But he would have to move on if she did.

'Of course, I would love to go to see a picture with you, Mr Howard, or I mean Noel,' Emily said giving him an even broader smile.

He held out his hand to shake her hand. They both felt it. Emily jumped back. It was like an electric current going through them.

'Well then, I look forward to seeing you on Friday night, Emily,' he said with a smile as he walked over to his jeep and headed back to the farm.

All the girls were in total shock. Was this a miracle, or what?! They all jumped around with excitement like a bunch of children who had just been given a bag of sweets.

Noel was whistling as he washed his hands, his mother giving out to him for not wiping his boots, the muck all over her clean floor. She hadn't seen him like that in a long time. It did her heart good to see her son in such good form once again. She wondered what had brought it about. Maybe Dublin had done him good after all. Noel's father was also delighted with the change in his son.

There was great excitement in the O'Hara house on Friday night. The girls were helping to dress Emily for the big night. Siobhan loaned her a beautiful orange satin dress and matched it with cream shoes and a purse that belonged to Emily.

'Maybe I'm a bit over dressed for a picture show?' Emily said.

'Emily, you could never be over dressed no matter what the occasion is,' Ellen told her.

Noel knocked on the front door of the O'Hara farm at seven in the evening. Emily, trying not to let her excitement show, answered the door, feeling quite awkward and shy as she looked at Noel. She looked back over her shoulder and said goodbye to her worried parents. At that very moment, Emily wished one of her friends was beside her. She felt like she needed to be doused with cold water, just to get some sort of sense back into her silly head.

Noel helped her into his jeep.

'First stop is a malt milkshake! Is that alright with you Emily?' he asked.

'Of course, it is,' said she, trying not to sound too eager. Secretly it wouldn't have made a daisy odds where they went as far as she was concerned.

Noel and Emily talked about everything. They spoke about everything that was happening in the parish and beyond. They seemed to have so much in common. Emily reminded Noel that they would miss the picture show if they didn't get a move on. But they just kept talking and the night just raced by.

'So, we have missed the picture, Emily,' said Noel eventually, 'but we will catch up on another show again, do you think?'

When he was leaving her home, he told her that he'd had a lovely evening and he hoped that she had enjoyed herself too. He added that he was delighted to get to know her.

'If it's alright with you Emily, I'd like to call on you again?' he said. She nodded her head as she closed her front door.

Noel called on Emily's father to make it official and ask if he could court his daughter.

'Well now, Noel, I would be a bit worried. I can't see you two being a match. I suppose it would be alright if you were friends and you treat my daughter with the utmost respect and your intentions are honourable.'

The Honourable Man

On Sunday night, Noel was standing at Emily's door, holding a bunch of pink roses. Erin O'Hara was delighted for her daughter at her seeing such a nice young gentleman.

In the Howard household, all was not well. Emily wouldn't be welcome in this house.

'You know we can't have this at all, son,' Noel's father said. 'You are wasting her time and yours making promises you won't be able to keep. You need to step back before it gets out of hand altogether. You may let her down as gently as possible,' continued his father in an angry voice. 'We don't want to make enemies in the parish, do you understand me, Noel?'

Noel could feel his father's anger. He wanted Noel to meet up in Dublin again with Winifred, a family friend of his cousin's. One of his own kind, as his father would say. Could he try and make a go of it with her? They had dated a couple of times but he just knew he would never love her. Not like the love he felt for Emily, he told his friend Jack. It had helped that he liked Winifred. She was a very nice girl. And the fact that she came from a moneyed background was also a big plus.

'You could never have enough money to run a farm well with all the new machinery coming on to the market,' he told Jack. 'It would be a perfect match, if only.'

'Don't worry for now, Noel,' said Jack, trying to talk some sense to Noel in the farmyard. 'You have plenty of time. Don't be in such a rush to get married.'

Noel knew Winifred would have jumped at a proposal if he asked her, but it wouldn't be fair to her. His heart didn't skip a beat when he was with her. It was more of a comfortable situation in her company, though they had only known each for a short time. But what was he to do? Should he let logic rule? He knew in his head what must be done!

It was just about settled in his head. He didn't want to string Emily along anymore. He decided to go to his uncle's farm in Dublin for a weekend to see Winifred so he could make up his mind. There was no question about his not loving Emily. They both just wouldn't stand a chance, not a hope, with all the pressure his father and his family, was putting on him.

Noel hadn't gotten in touch with Emily for three weeks. He was feeling guilty for asking her father to take her out. Emily could not understand what had happened. She thought they had gotten on very well.

'But not well enough,' Emily said to Siobhan. 'What was that all about? Noel asking her father if he could take her out? Why did he go to that trouble if his intentions were not serious? This is all so confusing,' she went on. 'I just know that he loves me! I can feel it in my bones.'

Emily also knew it was most likely that his family had a problem with her, well not her perhaps, but her Catholic background. How could she have ever thought it would have worked out at all, with such a divide between them and us?

An Upsetting Time in the Howard Household

The past three weekends Noel had spent his time back up on his cousin's farm.

'There has to be someone else,' said Siobhan. 'He is spending a lot of time out of the parish lately.'

The girls were trying to analyse the whole sorry saga between themselves.

So, Noel decided to let logic decide and asked Winifred to marry him. He didn't want to miss this chance of what was seen as a good match according to his parents. Some other farmer might have grabbed her if he didn't hurry as he was sure Winifred would get plenty of offers.

Noel rang home to tell his family the good news.

'One of our own kind,' they said. 'There will be a party in this house when you come home son, with your lovely girl. We just can't wait to meet her Noel. We are over the moon. I'm sure her family is very happy for their daughter, my son, she is getting a fine man. You take after your father and are a good hardworking and thoughtful person.'

Noel didn't feel kind and considerate like his father after letting Emily down without any explanation at all. He had let the love of his life go, the only girl he had ever lost sleep over. Those feelings just wouldn't leave him.

It was like a woodpecker on his head and that wouldn't stop pecking. He was in more of a predicament than ever. Was he making the right decision? But at the same time, he knew what had to be done. It would be best for both families in the end.

Madge heard the news in the shop. Noel's mother told her how delighted they all were at Noel's engagement to Winifred. Madge felt her stomach lurch and was quite queasy as she thought of Emily. After all, Emily was like a daughter to her. How was she going to take this at all?

Turmoil for Emily

Word reached Emily's house. Her friends were shocked to say the least and were very upset for her. She locked herself away in her room and no amount of coaxing to get her out would work. It went on for days. Something had to be done. Emily's mother, Erin, sent for Siobhan. She was so worried for her poor daughter, if she could take the pain of such rejection she would in a heartbeat. She felt helpless for her heartbroken child. She was taking Noel's engagement so very hard.

Emily finally opened the door to Siobhan. She was white as snow. Her eyes were red and swollen. She fell on the bed crying. It seemed impossible for someone to have so many tears.

'I really thought we would get together at the right time. I was prepared to wait forever if I had to. We got on so well. I just don't understand, Siobhan,' she cried. 'What will I do? I feel so sick. There is such a thing as love at first sight and it happened for Noel and me. I just can't get my head around it.'

Siobhan was broken-hearted for her friend and couldn't quite believe what had happened.

The Wedding Invitation

The cream and primrose invitations were sent out to Noel's relatives and friends:

Robert and Bertha Rothwell, would like Mr and Mrs Bernard
Byrne, to join in the marriage celebrations of their daughter
Winifred to Mr Noel Howard.

The day arrived for Noel's family to visit the Rothwell household to meet all the family. Winifred held Noel's hand with sheer delight and kissed him on the cheek. He was happy in a comfortable kind of way. Both sets of parents got on so well. 'I think I have made the right choice,' he thought to himself. If only my heart would agree with my head.

Noel pulled up outside Madge's shop and went inside for a couple of messages for his mother. She didn't have a minute to spare, he told Madge, with all the preparations for the wedding. Madge greeted him as she always did, not showing she was broken-hearted for Emily.

When he was leaving the shop, he shouted back, 'See you and Bernard at the wedding!'

He almost knocked over Siobhan and Charlotte at the shop door. All three were very embarrassed.

'I'm so sorry girls,' said Noel. 'But can I ask you how Emily is doing?'

'Very well, thank you for asking,' said Siobhan. 'Don't worry, Noel. You weren't dating for very long, and Emily is seeing someone else now and is happy. She has no intention of settling down for a very long time. She will have many a bow before she does.'

The girls wouldn't tell Emily that they met Noel, but were as mad as hell with him for having led her on.

A Happy Time

Before Noel knew it, the big day had arrived. His father and mother were in great form. Noel and his father had so much to do, what with hiring in help and organising the farm for the couple of days. Finally, he was ready and was looking forward to marrying Winifred. He had spent every second weekend in Dublin for the last couple of months.

His mother would tell Madge that his feet were well and truly under the Rothwell table, and that they were delighted with the match. He had spent enough time moping around and now he was happy.

'Isn't it awful what the heart can do to a person?' Noel's mother went on, 'and in most cases, you have to let the head rule and not the heart, don't you think Madge? That's how a good match is usually made.'

'I wouldn't know about that at all,' answered Madge, 'with Bernard and myself never having any children of our own, so I'm not sure how either of us would react to what might be a good or bad match.'

CHAPTER THREE

Time Out for a Friend in Need

It was time for some drastic action. Charlotte suggested to the girls that they go down to Cork for the weekend of Noel's marriage. They all agreed it was a good idea and wondered why they hadn't thought of it before.

'Maybe Emily would have perked up a lot earlier, but it is never too late, so let's get started,' said Charlotte.

The girls had some friends from their college years living and working in Cork who were only too happy accompany the girls to a charity ball, which was being held in the Metropole Hotel. Emily's friends set about making it a memorable night for everyone, especially Emily. The night proved a huge success, with everyone admiring all the glamour and the girls enjoying the champagne and the canapés. All were as happy as they could be, considering the situation. Siobhan even managed to make Emily laugh. The girls thought that maybe Emily has turned a corner and would get back to her old self again.

The next morning was spent shopping with endless cups of tea and cream pastries.

'Not a time for dieting!' said Charlotte, as she dug in to her second cream cake. One of Emily's purchases was a beautiful red dress made of pure silk. The girls admired the dress on her.

'Well, you are a picture, Em!' said Charlotte, speaking to her broken-hearted friend. 'It's lovely to see some colour back in your cheeks again.'

The girls formed a circle and gave each other a group hug, jumping up and down as they did.

'The weekend isn't over till tomorrow!' said Charlotte. 'We're going to the picture house tonight, so we will have an early dinner before we go. Maybe we'll meet up with the lads for a drink in the hotel after the pictures? What do you think girls? We won't be down here for a while again so let's make the best of it!'

Charlotte was the right person for the job. She had everything worked out right down to the last little detail, and all the girls were very thankful.

'When we get home, we must buy Charlotte a bunch of nice flowers for being so considerate,' said Siobhan, and they all agreed.

Three Broken Hearts

After having a glass of sherry, Noel and his parents decided to call it a night. After all they couldn't keep everyone up, especially Winifred.

'She'll need her beauty sleep if she's to look well in her beautiful dress on the day of all days, her wedding day,' said Noel's mother, giving her future daughter-in-law a big hug. 'Dying to see you in the morning, Winifred!'

Noel gave his bride a long lingering kiss. It didn't matter if the parents were watching. Of course, everyone was delighted to see so much affection between the two of them.

'Indeed, we'll have plenty of grandchildren if this carries on,' said the parents.

Back at the hotel everyone was in top form. There was a strong pot of tea for mum and a whiskey for Noel, his father and Jack, his best man.

Everyone was in good form the next morning. The only thing missing were flowers for the buttonholes. Noel's mother would ring Winifred's mother first thing to sort it out. There was nothing to worry about.

All arrived at the church in good time. Noel's mother was wearing a salmon pink outfit and a string of pearls to set it off, with tiny pearl earrings to match. Winifred's mother wore blue silk and a large hat with a few feathers sticking up. Her husband had a go at her.

'The poor pheasant will die of the cold!'
Madge and Bernard gave the family a set of silver cutlery and wished Noel well. She whispered to her husband, 'We simply cannot go to the wedding! So, we will give a good excuse as to why not.'

'Don't worry,' said Bernard, 'with the shop, they'll understand how hard it is to take time off.'

Other business people in the parish gave expensive gifts to the family.

Good customers in the parish, everyone that counted, all dug deep in their pockets for Noel and his family.

A Marriage of Convenience

The organ was playing. Everyone had taken their seats. Noel sat in the pew with his best man, Jack. He felt sick. When he kissed Winifred last night, nothing happened. He didn't want stars, or explosions, but he knew comfortable wouldn't cut it at all. This was going to be a marriage of convenience for him. He knew that Winifred loved him. So, could he go through with it? Could they make it work?

'For God's sake Jack! What am I going to do? How will I make a go of this marriage at all?' he said. 'I've made a right fecking mess of it and will only end up resenting her in time to come. I should love her,' he went on, 'she's a lovely woman, so what is it? Don't marriages like this work all the time, Jack?'

'Noel, there's no getting out of this now,' said a concerned Jack. 'Look around at all these happy faces. No, my very good friend, you must bite the bullet. You'll never be forgiven —'

But before Jack had finished the sentence, Noel was up and out of his seat, making his way out the side door and straight over to Winifred.

Winifred's bridesmaid was arranging her dress. She knew straight away that something wasn't right. She thought after that passionate kiss last night that he loved her, and went to bed dreaming of a lovely future together. If he only gave them both a chance she would make him a good wife! She just couldn't bear to hear what she was about to hear.

'Winifred,' he began to plead with her, 'we can't do this. You need a man who loves you. You deserve better! Especially when I'm in love with someone else! I've tried so hard. I like you so very much, but it is not love, not love at all.'

She could feel herself about to faint. With the help of her bridesmaid she stayed upright. She wondered if this was a dream and thought, this can't be happening.

'But Noel, I love you. Please, please, give me a chance! Give us both a chance.'

Tears streamed down both their faces.

'Ah, Winifred! You can say you called the wedding off and I will be the jilted one. I am the one to be upset, not you,' Noel went on. 'You wouldn't want to live with someone who does not really love you with all his heart? Please forgive me for leaving it so long and causing this pain.'

He turned around to find his friend Jack at his side.

'Winifred, I am so sorry for you both,' said Noel's friend, putting his arms around the two of them. 'I will take care of everything.'

Jack made his way back in to the church after having a quite word with Vicar Montrose, and made his way up to the altar. The bridesmaid, who was in a total state of shock, tried to comfort her best friend. She confessed to Winifred that she had had concerns about Noel's true feelings for her.

'You said to me on a few occasions about him never telling you that he loved you. You never heard these words come from his mouth, even though you told him that you loved him so very much.'

'But I thought Noel might not able to express his true feelings for me,' answered Winifred, 'you know how some men are.'

'Winifred, I think you were settling and that would have been an awful mistake, when the right man is out there somewhere for you, my poor Winifred, my best friend!'

And both friends started to cry again.'

Jack made his announcement to the guests.

'It is with regret I have to tell you that this wedding will not now take place as both the bride and groom have decided to call off their wedding today. I, as best man, apologise to our Vicar Montrose, and all the guests on behalf of the couple.'

After apologising to everyone, he went down to the distraught parents to explain what had happened. Needless to say, the bride's family were more than upset with Noel and his family. Jack explained to Winifred's parents that the Howard family would pay for any expenses incurred for the wedding. And once again, Noel kept saying how sorry he was to Winifred, sorry that he hadn't told her earlier. Even last night would have saved face for her.

The Howard family checked out of the hotel after paying the bill for the wedding breakfast and the florist. They would arrange payment for the rest later. On the way home, everyone was upset. Noel's mother was crying. She had become very fond of Winifred, who by then, had been calling her Mother Howard. They had so much in common, from quilting to knitting, to swapping recipes.

'She is just a lovely girl in every way,' said Miriam.

There was some serious talking done on the way home.

'But son, for goodness sake! Why didn't you tell her before you both had organised everything?'

'I was in it too deep,' Noel answered, 'and hadn't the heart to tell her. I thought we could make it work to please everyone and it would be a match that suited both families.'

Jack had a calming effect on everyone.

'Let's stop in the next town and have a bit to eat, and some strong tea and coffee. What do you think?'

They all agreed straight away. The rest of the relatives and the guests from the parish followed them to the hotel. Everyone tried to make sense of it all, but no one judged Noel. If there was going to be a problem down the line, now was the time to sort it out.

'Jack, what an awful mess! And all because I couldn't make up my mind and left it way too late!'

Jack knew his friend well and saw that Noel had lost heart a long time ago, and that Winifred wasn't the one for him.

'I should have sat you both down together last night,' said Jack, 'to make sure that you both were happy with no problems facing either one of you. Maybe then you could have avoided this dreadful situation.'

Jack headed to the bar and returned with three strong whiskeys for Noel, his father and himself. If there ever was a time for a stiff drink, now was it. All three men knocked back the whiskey.

News spread like wildfire through the village and beyond the whole parish. Madge and Bernard couldn't believe it. There would be plenty of talk going on for a long time to come. Emily wasn't entirely upset. She wondered if it all meant that he loved her. But at the same time, she felt so sorry for his bride, left standing at the altar.

'If he could do that to her, what does it say about him?' she said to Erin.

Emily's friends were amazed. They knew now for sure that Noel didn't love Winifred and that Emily must be the one! Things would become clear after all the fuss had died down. Madge was helping the friends to come to terms with this not complete catastrophe, where Noel had followed his heart. Madge asked Noel's mother how she felt about the postponement of the wedding while in the shop doing her shopping.

'Oh, Madge! We are all in shock. If only he had told her earlier,' she went on, 'and had not left it until the last minute. It would have been a lot better on all of us. We have been very busy Madge, with wrapping up the wedding presents to send them all back.'

Madge felt sorry for Winifred, for the embarrassment she must have felt, and had no problem saying it to Noel's mother.

'Madge, we should have pulled back a long time ago and let him go for the girl he loves. So, we must take some of the blame! For that I am sorry, and poor Winifred wouldn't have gone through this awful time. I don't mind telling you how devastated we are,' said Noel's mother. She continued, 'I know you don't go talking about what goes on in people's private lives and are a woman you can trust, and I thank you for that Madge. It has been a hard few weeks for both families, but I have no doubt we will get through it. Noel is feeling just awful about the whole thing. He is working like a Trojan and can't be stopped. Sure, we had to call Jack over to talk sense into him.'

The Waiting

After a couple of months Noel wondered how long more would he have to wait until he met up with Emily again. This time, he thought to himself almost out loud, he would never let her go. He needed to believe that Emily felt the same way about him. He longed to hold and kiss her, but he knew he would have to wait another while. He had held her in his heart for what seemed forever, waiting for the woman he loved, and he knew for sure he would never love another.

Who Were They to Tell Their Children Who to Love

Noel finished up on the farm earlier than expected and was glad it was the weekend. There was not much time off where farming was concerned, but it was a bit more relaxed on weekends. He only hoped that there would be no emergency.

Noel's father felt sorry for his son, and apologised once again for the whole fiasco that they had caused, by forcing him towards Winifred. Noel's parents were prepared to listen to what he had to say, but also explained to Noel that they couldn't possibly have had Emily come and live in this house.

'After all she is not of our faith, son,' said his father. 'If you decide to marry this girl you will have to leave the farmhouse and move down to the village to rent or buy a house. We as a family will have to work out our differences somehow.'

Emily's people helped the Howard family out with the harvest every year, as did everyone else at this busy time. All got on well together, with plenty of grub supplied by the women of the house, and Emily and Noel's people tried to put aside their differences.

'Both the Howard and O'Hara families will cross this very difficult bridge if it happens,' said Madge to Bronwyn. 'But for everyone's sake, both sets of parents hope it won't and are totally against this marriage.'

The Proposal

Noel called his friend Jack to meet him in Johnny's pub for a pint of Guinness. He told his friend of his intentions to propose to Emily.

'It's long overdue, don't you think, my friend?' said Noel to Jack.

After twenty minutes or so Jack gave up trying to stop him, all his arguing falling on deaf ears.

Noel hopped into his jeep and drove to Emily's house. The journey seemed to take forever. He knocked on the door as hard as he could.

'Noel! You will bring the house down for goodness sake!' said John O'Hara, Emily's father.

As John enquired if everyone over at the farm was alright, Emily passed behind her father and looked over his shoulder to see Noel. At that moment, she knew what he wanted to ask her! He dropped down on one knee.

'Emily Anne O'Hara, this time will you be the love of my life and only you?'

Emily was still hurting and was afraid to trust him.

'Please Noel, I need to think about it! I have been in love with you for a long time, from that first night at the dance. I was heartbroken thinking you could just go off and get married to someone else! I couldn't understand it Noel!' she continued, 'after you asking my father to court me. I thought you felt the same about me. You led me to believe it to be so. Then to go off and marry someone else just like that! What a monstrous way to treat me. So, for the moment Noel, you will have to wait for my answer.'

'But Emily!' Noel replied. 'I thought that the difference in our religion would stop us from being together and cause hardship on our families. Please forgive me for breaking your heart. I never meant to cause you pain.'

'Not just me,' said Emily, 'you caused another girl great pain, and at the church altar, Noel.'

'Noel, you will have to go,' said Emily's annoyed father. 'Emily is not ready for this yet, or any of us for that matter.'

'Maybe you and me can never be together after this awful mess,' sighed Emily. 'Your family won't want me and I can't blame them, after all that has happened.'

Noel spoke to Emily in a low voice as he made his way out the front door and looked at her tenderly, with tears in his eyes,

'I'll give you time, Emily.'

Jack knocked on Emily's door a couple of months later.

'Please Mr O'Hara, can I speak to Emily, if you don't mind?'

'Not at all son, come in to the parlour. God, there is an awful lot of traffic altogether in this house tonight,' said John O'Hara, under his breath. 'Brendan Redmond is here to ask Emily if she will go to a picture show. I will check if she will see you Jack. Is this about Noel? She needs time, son,' Emily's father continued, 'but I will call my daughter anyway and maybe the woman of the house will bring in a drop of tea for you.'

Emily excused herself from Brendan saying maybe another night she would go to the cinema, but at the moment she was not up to seeing anyone. Then she went to sit down beside Jack and listened to what he had to say for an hour or more and a second pot of tea. Jack had told her everything that had happened and how it would never have worked out with Winifred.

'What he went through on the last few days leading up to the wedding was just awful,' he said. 'You see, Emily, where the heart is concerned there is just nothing you can do about it. I do believe that you and Noel are meant to be together and there is no other person on this whole earth for either one of you.'

She agreed with him but was nervous about taking this first step. But every time she thought of Noel, that same old feeling was still there in her stomach. Jack caught hold of her hand as both made their way outside.

'Emily, Noel is out here waiting in his jeep,' Jack told her.

He had been waiting and waiting for what seemed like hours. One way or another Noel was going to fight for his sweetheart, the love of his life.

The Match

Emily and Noel talked way into the night, drinking endless cups of tea. Then it was time for Noel to make his way home. He drew Emily close and gave her a long and tender kiss. Both were overwhelmed by emotion and knew without a shadow of doubt there would never be anyone else.

It was eleven in the morning on a Saturday. Noel called to pick Emily up. Erin O'Hara was more than concerned for what might be facing the young couple, but was glad for her daughter, glad they had finally gotten together at last. But the same cannot be said of her father, who wondered how on earth his brother, Fr Rory, would take all of it.

The happy couple went over to Rayland's jewellery shop in Wicklow to buy the biggest ring that would fit on Emily's finger. She picked a ring with an emerald green stone set in the middle of two diamonds. Money wasn't going to be an issue as far as Noel was concerned. He could never make it up to Emily, after the heartache he had caused her. Her cheeks were glowing and she looked beautiful, dressed in a green dress with sleeves that stopped midway down her arms. Erin had put a tiny vintage blue broach on her daughter's dress. It was her special piece, which an elderly aunt had given to her on her engagement to Emily's father.

Emily and Noel kissed tenderly, the shop owner looking on at the blissful couple. How could he have known what a predicament this young couple found themselves in? Picture perfect, the young couple then made their way to G.J. Hoer's photography studio.

On the way home, Madge was the first person they visited to show the ring.
'Imagine that! Me, your first call?'
'You know, Madge, that you are like a second mother to me,' said Emily. 'My father won't even entertain the idea of this marriage. You are the first to be told.'
Then the girls were told. Her friends were beside themselves with excitement.
Emily and Noel's friends organised a party for the couple: Sunday evening at seven for tea and something to eat in the Quaker hall. Fr Rory O'Hara and Reverend Isaac Howard were more than upset at Emily and Noel, for not picking someone from their own faith, both clergy spitting fire at each other, saying that this wouldn't do at all!
Siobhan ordered the engagement cake from Alice Molten, who was renowned for her confectionery. Emily's mother arrived at the party with Madge and Bronwyn, all three bringing savoury and sweet dishes. Jack and the girls put on a good spread for their friends. Emily's father and Noel's parents did not make an appearance at the party. All stayed at home in disgust.
It was a few weeks after the engagement. Noel knew he had no choice but to move out of his home. He finished most of the morning chores on the farm, and made his way in to the house. It was time to have the talk he had been dreading with his parents. He couldn't stick the silence any longer. He explained how he would be taking up digs along with one of the local bank clerks in the boarding house down in the village. He told them that it would be best for everyone for the time being, and that it wouldn't affect his work on the farm.

His father did not speak while his mother tried to hide her tears at the embarrassment of it all. Though hoping all would go well in the boarding house, they did not ask after Emily at all.

Bronwyn informed Noel and Emily of a vacant house not too far from her own home. It belonged to the Roger family who had emigrated to America the previous year and one of the relatives was selling the house on their behalf.

'It will need a good deal of work done on it,' Bronwyn said, 'but it's not bad at all. It has plenty of garden and is close to everyone. There's not a chance of getting lonely, Emily,' said Bronwyn with a smile.

'Emily, what do you think?' asked Noel.

'I think it is just what the doctor ordered for you and me,' answered Emily, 'away from the parents with no pressure on us as we start our life together.'

A House of Our Own

Michael Barnes, a reputable builder, was employed for the job, along with Barry Barnes a top carpenter. Martin Marlow, the plumber, and James Mc-Grath, the local electrician, would also work on the house. Lisa Marlow would help Emily to paint and wallpaper. Siobhan made up the curtains for the house and Erin, Emily's mother, had cream blinds fitted on all the windows. It was a lovely home for newlyweds.

Of course, not all was well in the Howard household. In the O'Hara's, Emily's father was beginning to accept Noel as his future son-in-law.

'Sure, I couldn't hold a grudge against him,' he told his wife. 'If he is good enough for my daughter he is good enough for me. Besides, I like the lad, so I do.'

The Wedding Day Finally Arrives

With a year behind them, a date was finally set for the wedding. As far as Emily's friends were concerned, it was game, set and match. Siobhan was to be Emily's witness. She wore a mid-length pink silk dress with cream rose-petals around the neckline, which complimented Emily's short-sleeved cream lace dress, showing off her beautiful gold watch, which was a wedding present from Noel on this special day. Emily also bought her fiancé a set of gold cufflinks with his initials engraved in them along with, *Love from Em*, on the back.

Jack was to be Noel's witness.

'No cold feet now, Noel' he joked. He knew for sure they were the perfect match, despite the differences in their religion and the trouble it has caused that might never be put right.

An Early Start

Their appointment at the registry office in Dublin was to take place at eleven o'clock sharp. The wedding party would have to reach Dublin by no later than 9am.

Noel's father only spoke to his son on matters that had to do with the farm. He couldn't stomach this ill-fated match and by not speaking to Noel at all, he was making his point quite clear. This stand-off had had a wearing effect on Noel. Emily was so upset that she had caused such a rift amongst the families. Hardly anyone was speaking to each other. The strong women of the parish, Erin, Emily's mother, and Madge and Bronwyn were all trying to coax them to make it up with the young couple, but there was no budging Noel's father.

'It looks like it will be a good sunny day for this July wedding,' said Erin O'Hara to Madge and Bernard. 'It will be a happy day for everyone involved.'

Noel and Emily had decided not to get married in either church, as they had no intention on bringing the fire of the parents down on either of them. They had sat both sets of parents down a few days after they got engaged, to clear up any confusion about the wedding plans.

'It's going to be in a registry office,' said Noel, 'with Siobhan and Jack as our witnesses. When we get back from Dublin we will have a small party for the people that matter most to us, and who stood by us.'

He gave a reassuring hug to Emily.

Bronwyn, the parish nurse, was doing her shopping in Madge's when Erin appeared, looking tired and pale with dark circles around her eyes. Bronwyn told her that she could be lacking in iron.

'You need get a check-up by the doctor, Erin.'

'Emily and Noel are having an awful rough time of it and it is taking its toll on me,' she said to Bronwyn. 'They think that my Emily is not good enough for them. My Emily?!'

Madge's blood started to boil with rage at the stand-off. 'A cut above buttermilk, she thought? They don't amount to much in mine or Bernard's eyes! And we thought we knew them? As they say, you only get to really know someone in a time of crisis.

Better Late Than Never

Noel's mother ran into the registry office, calling out, 'Am I too late?'

The registrar put a finger on his mouth and pointed at a vacant seat. Erin rose and threw her arms around Noel's mother and both mothers cried for their children.

Madge and Bernard were top of the guest list. Along with Bronwyn, they knew just about everyone in the parish. There was a good mix of guests, people of all faiths together, at ease in each other's company. They included Johnny and Rose Mythen who were very popular publicans that were always very involved with everyone on market day.

All Noel could spare was a week off for the honeymoon. Some local lads helped his father out on the farm.

Emily explained to Madge how she couldn't wait to move in to their house and her mother was sending over some pieces of furniture from her home. One of the pieces was a rosewood table.

'Now that's what I call a present!' said Noel to his excited wife.

Not to be left out, Noel's mother bought a cream, antique rose bowl as a centrepiece for the table, saying nothing to her angry husband, who if he had his way, would have had her not speaking to Noel either.

A New Addition

Emily Anne O'Hara was born on the 5 August 1928, and Noel Ivor Howard was born on 12 May 1923. Emily and Noel married in July 1954, and their first baby arrived in 1957. They both were very excited and looked forward to the birth of their first child and knew their lives would never be the same again. It wouldn't be at all easy to just grab a coat and go visiting family or friends at the drop of a hat. But they were thrilled at the thought of their lives being turned upside down. They had put off starting a family for a few years as they had wanted a precious couple of years for themselves.

Madge and Bernard always got on well with both families and were invited to both houses on many an occasion. They were an honorary part of their families, but this past while things had changed between them, and in the Howard household there was a slight coolness. Madge said to Bernard,

'Can't you feel it from Noel's father?'

Bernard tried to explain how Bertie Howard had nothing against the O'Hara family but thought it always better for people to stick to their own faith. But his argument was to no avail and Miriam and Madge were both embarrassed by this ridiculous conversation. Bernard said to Madge later, 'It's like talking to a wall. Bertie Howard has his mind made up and no one was going to change it for him. Not even John O'Hara.'

The whole parish could feel the pressure of the stand-off between Noel and his father, and Noel's uncle, the Vicar. It had taken its toll on just about everyone.

'It's going on far too long now, Bernard,' said Madge, 'we need to do something about it.'

'But what?' asked Bernard.

Noel decided Monday would be a good day to take off. He knew he couldn't just head off at the drop of a hat. But his father could ask young Miley from the neighbouring farm to come over for the day to help with the livestock. Miley was always happy to oblige, glad of that extra money. Emily also took time out from the household chores, glad of the chance of an outing with Noel that would do them both good. Emily was a country girl at heart. The only time she spent away from home was when she was in college in Dublin. She had always looked forward to coming home at weekends. She liked the odd day trip to the big city, but it rarely ever happened these days. She was so busy all the time, helping on her father's farm, that there was always plenty to be done. She also had to make time to help with local fundraising for the local charities, and also for Africa. Emily loved this busy life of hers, especially when it included her husband Noel, who was always helping someone out on one farm or another if any one of them ran into problems. They always had plenty to talk about over dinner. Emily got on well with everyone when teaching the younger children. Everyone could get on with Emily, she had a good kind heart. Nothing was a problem to her at all if she could help.

Time Out for the Two of them

'I'll take this opportunity to do some shopping for the baby and have a nice tea on the way home,' Emily thought to herself. She felt just because they were married and expecting their first child, it didn't have to mean the honeymoon was over. As far as she was concerned, she was always going to make her Noel feel special, like he was the most important man in the world. In fact, he really was, in her world. Emily still felt that flutter of excitement whenever he whispered sweet nothings in her ear. She would think how lucky she was to have found such a kind loving man, and not just kind to her. He never begrudged giving his time to whoever might need it.

'He didn't pick that up off the floor. His father is the very same,' the locals would say. 'He would do a good turn for anyone. Now look at the division their marriage has caused.'

Noel had some business to do in one of the large co-ops on Capel Street in Dublin. Noel of course always believed in keeping local businesses going. The local lads would do anything for you. But it wasn't always possible to buy local. He was delighted when Emily decided to come along for the trip.

Noel could listen to her talking all day long. She had an opinion on all the news, be it big or small in the parish. Emily liked order in her life. She knew how to make their home warm and welcoming and to feel lived-in, like a home should feel. But not too neat! It was important that her husband could walk in to his house with his wellingtons on, though not in the lovely parlour! She knew she would have to draw the line somewhere.

Fuel for the Body

Emily never ceased to surprise her husband. At least four times a year, she would make plans, with the help of Noel's mother, for her son to have an overnight break away when he would not have to return until the following evening. But so much organising was needed to bring in an extra pair of hands on the farm. Only then could Noel relax and be happy, knowing that the farm was in safe hands. His mother made sure his father would not be under too much pressure.

Emily always had plenty to talk about. She was very good at sorting out other people's problems, giving them the best advice she could, and demonstrating both the teacher and counsellor in her.

A New Chapter in Noel and Emily's Life

There was so much to choose from the gorgeous ranges of baby clothes. Of course, both grandmothers had plenty of clothes put away in suitcases and chests in the attic, not to mention prams and cots. But Emily wanted to buy some nice new pieces of clothing for their first-born child. It was going to be an exciting time for them both. Emily wandered around the shops wondering if she should buy pink or blue. It would be awful to get it wrong! Or maybe, she thought, she should play it safe and buy yellow and white. But she felt sure she was going to have a boy. Wasn't everybody telling her she was carrying high, so it was most definitely a boy. Being a first-time mother, she took their word for it, sure she knew nothing about babies.

Alice Molten was very fond of the Howard family. She ran the local bakery and always boasted about her lovely cakes for every occasion. Her reputation preceded her. Madge and Emily's mother, Erin, both agreed she was a very important woman in the parish. Alice insisted on making the christening cake as a gift for Emily and Noel's first baby. She asked Emily what colour she would like. If Emily was sure that she was going to have a boy, it absolutely should be blue and white. But Alice wasn't sure at all. What if Emily was wrong? But after much thought, Alice decided to follow Emily's wishes and hoped she was right.

'Maybe she has some sort of sixth sense?' she said to Madge. 'Sure, don't you often hear people talking about such things? Well, time will tell. For her sake, I only hope she is right.'

Alice was half hoping Madge would have some miraculous advice.

Noel worked on a mixed farm of a thousand acres or thereabouts. He made a good living, what with keeping pigs, chickens and geese. They were well able to do business with the local shops, selling their bacon, milk, eggs and vegetables, and also did a good Christmas trade in selling turkeys, geese and ham for the festive season. Noel's mother and father had worked all their married lives on the farm, with little time off. But they always felt it was important to put time aside to bring their young son to some of the parish activities, and to get him involved in rugby, football or horse riding. Noel was always a very outgoing boy, well able to mix with the other boys. The Howard family were very good farmers who didn't leave an acre unused. Noel's grandfather had been well known as one of the best farmers for miles around, and a decent man to all the hired help.

Emily was required by the State to give up her teaching post when she married, but that didn't stop her helping in the school if one of the teachers went out. She was happy enough to keep a hand in. Why wouldn't she? After all, she didn't become a teacher just to give it up! She had always wanted to make a difference to the young children in her charge, and was glad to be called on to stand in.

Before she married, she taught children from the ages of four to twelve years old. Emily knew just about everybody, from the well-off to the not so well-off. Some children who needed help came to school grubby because they were rarely washed. They were hardly fed, the poor little things, and were hungry most of the time. Emily knew it was impossible to help all of them. There was only so much a teacher could do. She knew what fate awaited these children: hard work, low-paid jobs, no self-worth and a total lack of confidence. Their parents did not realise at all how important it was for the children to do homework every evening, so they could achieve and be the best they could be. Emily knew that some of the brightest of these students would go on and do their very best to get an education, and that they just might make it. But of course, everything depended on their family and the interest shown in their children's education.

CHAPTER FOUR

Their Protégée

Margaret Gaynor was a very bright young student. She was very inquisitive and was always asking questions. She had a love for English and history, and never wanted the class to end. Some of the kinder teachers kept an eye on the young girl throughout her primary school years, doing whatever they could for her, and any other youngster who appeared to have a love for learning. But not all the teachers bothered with these little souls. Not that they didn't want to help, but they just saw most cases as hopeless.

Emily and Charlotte took a great interest in this young girl Margaret. Between them they would make her their protégée! They gave young Margaret extra time, and thought maybe just maybe they would or could pull another youngster out of the poverty trap, putting a fire under their young charge to make something out of her life. Before Emily left to get married, she made a promise to take the young girl up to her home a couple of evenings a week for an hour to continue to educate her. Both young teachers shook hands on it.

The young educators put in a lot of work teaching her every subject she needed for secondary school. Emily and Charlotte supplied all the extra books and copies for Margaret and whatever else that she might need, with the help from Mother Veronica, a kind-hearted nun.

It was never a hard job teaching Margaret. She had a head for knowledge and never seemed tired, always willing to learn with a smile. She was a joy to work with and was an example of what teaching was all about. Emily and Charlotte spoke to each other about Margaret with a smile and a sense of achievement.

It was a time for Margaret on her own and away from her noisy family. She loved being with her favourite teachers. They made her feel special and usually gave her biscuits or a slice of madeira cake, and a glass of cold milk, every time she stayed on to do extra study. Charlotte bought her a bag of toiletries, explaining how to use them, and how to keep her school clothes clean and how to hand wash her underwear separately. Margaret would try and copy how Charlotte and Emily spoke, she looked up to the young teachers so much. She copied their basic manners, and how they treated and greeted people. Although she was young, Margaret had an old head. She was made to grow up fast in a very troubled household.

Margaret wondered why her mother had never taught her all this basic stuff. The more she learned, the more ignorant her family seemed to her. At home, she knew things weren't right. She couldn't understand why her father was always in a bad mood. Her older brother wasn't much better. He had no problem with belting her on the head and calling her names, such as Miss Fancy Pants and other rude names. It didn't matter what she said to him. Her mammy always gave out to him like anything, but all he would do was make fun of his mother. Margaret's daddy didn't mind one bit and never helped her at all. She just couldn't do anything about her circumstances.

Margaret worked in a small shop in the village a couple of evenings after school and every Saturday. The shop always seemed quite empty. There was not much stock kept on the shelves at all. The lady who owned the shop just kept a few groceries in for some of her family, who were farmers a few miles away. For the boss man, for his wife always addressed him by that name, Margaret would be sent over to Murphy's butcher shop across the street, for three slices of ham cut as thin as an English sixpence. The butcher usually laughed at her every time she asked for the ham. She got embarrassed each time and didn't understand what they were laughing at. Her job was cleaning two small bedrooms. Their son's bedroom was a little bigger than his mother's and his sisters'. She would scrub the spuds until they were almost shining and did everything else that needed doing to keep a house going. She would carry two steel buckets full of slops across the main street and over a large wall into what she thought was the main dump in town. By the time she emptied it out, her little arms were almost pulled out of her sockets.

Also on her list of chores was washing the old cement floor of the shop at eight on a Saturday night. It was a very long day. Sometimes she worked until ten o'clock. Sometimes even then, she would still find little jobs still to be done. Two shillings and sixpence was her pay from nine in the morning to late in the evening.

Margaret took her time walking from the shop up to the churchyard, which was about five minutes away, gathering all the courage she could muster. It was like getting ready for a race every Saturday.

Everybody said a house near the graveyard was haunted. Margaret made a run for it past the graveyard. She would stop for a couple of seconds, to catch her breath, but make sure that she was clear of danger. Then she would make another run for it, this time past a blue door set deep into a crumbling wall that stood at the side of a large house covered in creepers. The door led into an old garden. Some said a headless man stood in the doorway, so she made another run for it again away from the old haunted house. She would finally reach the top of her road, where the big black dog often appeared and was the devil himself.

With all that running and her being half-starved, there was not much food offered by the lady in the shop, except a few marietta biscuits and a small bottle of orange a couple of times in the day. She didn't feel much like eating anything when she got back home. She was only fit for her bed.

The terror she felt on her journey home would leave her shaken and the perspiration rolled down her body. Her mother would open the front door to her, holding her hand out for the money, which she then passed to the child's father, and him shouting, 'what took you so long?' Then he'd give her a slap on the side of her head. He would push past mother and child, on his way down to the local pub. Every Saturday was the same for Margaret, and nothing ever changed.

No Wisdom

Kitty told her children to keep quiet and not to make a sound, giving each of them a hug so they would feel safe. She had spent many years crying over her mistake in marrying Jerry, but she never let anyone see her in distress. She was very good at hiding how vulnerable she really was. At all times the children should feel safe, even if she was afraid herself. Kitty often wore a scarf to hide the bruises on her neck and face, and kept her arms well covered, never letting the people of the parish see how her husband was beating her. Sometimes she wondered if she might have provoked him and that maybe it was not always his fault.

Margaret's family couldn't possibly think of giving her a secondary education. In fact, it really annoyed them that she was spending so much time in school or with those know-it-all teachers in their houses, but her mother wouldn't let on to the teachers how she really felt about them and made out that she was glad of the interest they had shown in her daughter. Margaret's parents wanted her to work in the local houses cleaning and minding children. Her father couldn't wait for her to leave school at the tender age of twelve, not even thirteen, to bring home some much needed 'drinking money'.

'Sure, what would she need all that schooling for?' he would shout at his wife. 'Wasn't everybody belonging to her out working from a very young age. Hard work never did them any harm!'

How would the world carry on, Kitty would think to herself, if everybody worked in offices or fancy, highflying jobs? Surely houses, hotels, schools and restaurants have got to be cleaned by people like us? We help in keeping everything running smoothly for the people with the top jobs. We should be respected for the contribution we make to society. We are very important people indeed. Kitty just hoped her bright young daughter would do well. She was sure she would work her way up in any given job.

All Kitty's clothes shopping was done in a second-hand shop in Mary's Lane over in the next village. It was owned by a man called Patsy, who sold cheap clothes which Kitty hoped people wouldn't notice were second-hand. She always tried to better herself, sometimes looking at the way some of the well-off people dressed and how they communicated with each other. Every day was a lesson when Kitty learned something new. Whenever she spoke to her friend, she would encourage her to look and learn and told her that it was never too late to gain a bit more knowledge about how society worked.

What had she been thinking marrying such a man?! She wished with all her heart that she had had more wisdom and a better understanding of what life was about. She was seventeen at that time, too young to have made such an important decision for the rest of her life. She had felt sure then that her life would have been a lot better. Her husband had always been able to get around her in her younger years, always promising that things would improve.

She should have listened and have been guided by her loving parents, and her friends who had all warned her about him. Love is blind, so they say, and Kitty wouldn't listen, and so she found herself in a black tunnel with no way out. Now, she agreed with her friends, and could do nothing about her situation. Kitty had loved him or so she thought, mistaking a young girl's first crush. Trouble seemed to follow Jerry and she had thought nobody understood him like her, and that they were all wrong. But now every day was like walking in thick mud, each day a struggle for Kitty and her children.

CHAPTER FIVE

The Heart of the Community

A stream ran through the village of Kilton and there was a line of trees on either side of the main street. It looked so orderly, with four dark-green benches. Madge remembered when her friend Bronwyn had sat down on a summer evening not realising that the benches had just been freshly painted. The painter had forgotten to put the notice up saying 'wet paint'. Madge had come running out of her shop to warn her but it was too late, her nurse's uniform and the backs of her legs and hands now a deep green.

'Well, Bronwyn! You do look a sight,' said Madge, as she brought her friend to the back of the shop to clean her down. Drinking endless cups of tea, finally they removed all the paint with turpentine, leaving her legs quite raw and sore. She could hardly sit down after the whole sorry episode. Both women often laughed at what happened, but at the time it was no laughing matter at all.

There was a green and cream phone-box like a Sergeant Major at the end of the stream, where many a fight broke out when people spent too much time on a call. Bernard went out on quite a few occasions, if you could call it an occasion, to keep everyone calm when a fight broke out. But he wasn't always successful, he himself got threatened. Madge and the customers would watch from the shop door. Bernard and Madge's shop was at the top of the stream, so they had a good view of the goings-on in the town. The post office was also in Byrnes' shop. Madge and Bernard sold just about everything, from smoky bacon, poultry and everything else in-between, right down to balls of twine.

Everyone in the parish said that Madge was the salt of the earth. She understood most people's situations and trusted her own judgment about each one. If someone needed credit, she would never let a soul starve and only they would know about it and they were always very grateful.

Madge was in her fifties and often lamented not having children of her own. Her childbearing years had well passed her by. She had always longed to buy that beautiful christening robe, the lovely communion dress or the white suit with a striking blue tie. A wave of sadness washed over her when she caught sight of her wedding dress still hanging up in the back bedroom. Madge had almost forgotten how beautiful her wedding dress was. It had an amazing amount of delicate cream lace and tiny cream pearls around the neckline and on the end of the gown. It looked so graceful, it was hard for her to believe that she had fitted into such a gown all those years ago. The years have a way of putting a few pounds on a person, and before you know it you are buying bigger sizes without taking much notice. It was a true saying that you grow into comfort when you are happy, she thought.

Her mother had lovingly stitched a blue ribbon on the inside of the hem for good luck. Although it was well faded by now, it brought tears to her eyes just thinking of her mother and all the fuss that went on at the time of her wedding. Madge had hoped a daughter would have worn it on her wedding day. It had been her mother's. She remembered back to her beautiful wedding, when she was full of hopes and dreams, and a thrill of excitement rippled through her body of what tomorrow might bring. She could still feel that excitement now after all those years. She could still shed salty tears over what might have been. A daughter or son just wasn't meant to be.

A Time for Themselves

Bernard and Madge kept every Friday night free for themselves. Their lives were so busy it was hard to wind down. Both looked forward to sitting down to a fish supper. It was the one night they didn't have to scoff their dinner. Madge usually did her baking on a Thursday night, a couple of loaves of bread, which were a mix of brown and soda that would see them out through the week. There was nothing like her own bread. Bernard always said that you couldn't but have one when speaking of some fresh bread, the salty, country butter thickly spread on top. He'd say this repeatedly every Friday night and Madge would nod her head in agreement, as if she were hearing Bernard say those words for the very first time.

Bernard hung a sign on the shop door, written in large letters, which said, *Closed until eight thirty on Saturday morning.* If any of the locals ran out of something, they would just have to borrow from one of the neighbours. Under no circumstances would the shop door be answered. Business was discussed for a half an hour or so, and then it was on to more important things like listening to the wireless.

'Imagine hearing this all the way from England! Just imagine that Madge!' Bernard would say as they settled down to listen to what was happening on *The Archers.*

'It's hard to imagine they are ordinary people just like us, making a living as actors on the wireless,' Bernard would continue. 'Well now, Madge, I wouldn't say that about you, definitely not ordinary. You keep a lot of people going in the parish, whether it is selling them groceries, or having the auld chat and giving advice. No, Madge, you are definitely not ordinary! Nothing much changes. Whether on a radio talk show or anywhere else, everyone has problems at some stage in their lives.'

They would have plenty to talk about after listening to each episode, though they wouldn't always agree with each other. Bernard would have liked to give some of the characters a good telling-off, while Madge would pity some of them. Madge knew just how frustrated Bernard got if things did not run the way he would like them to. He must have order in the shop. If he had his way, every customer would have to form an orderly queue. But, of course, Bernard knew that his thinking was not right at all.

Bernard had been a sergeant in the army many years ago. It had been there that he learned how to have order in his life, from the smallest task, such as dressing his bed, to scrubbing out the mess, working his way up the ranks. He had worked from the time he got up in the morning to last thing at night. No matter how hard he tried now, he found it hard to leave it behind him.

'If only some of these gobshites and know-it-alls knew what it was really like to fight in a war for God-knows-what,' he'd say. 'If they saw just a little of what I have seen, then maybe they wouldn't be going around causing trouble and pitying themselves over nothing.'

But he knew that he must not take out his frustration on innocent people and let his anger spill out into his working life. That wouldn't have been good for business at all, but he still had no intention of suffering fools.

Madge had a calming effect on him. It had been what had attracted him to her in the first place. He had never met anyone quite like her. Bernard knew in his heart that he would never survive without his sweetheart and wasn't shy about telling her so. Everybody loved being in Madge's company. Her mood never changed, she always had a big smile on her face and made time for everyone. She believed everybody was born equal, and that it was unfortunate circumstances of their birth that often hindered people. Madge also believed that you should never look down on a poor soul unless you were giving them a hand up.

The same could not be said of her husband. Bernard had a good heart and would give very generously to people in need. But he could be very cranky at times; in fact he was always whining about one thing or another. People steered clear of him and most of the time they were relieved when he was not around.

Madge was a good businesswoman. Whether it was the bank manager or Kitty Gaynor, she treated everyone the same and couldn't do enough for her customers. People just loved chatting to her and she was never in a rush. If anyone was in a hurry, she packed up their shopping straight away. As her friend Bronwyn often told her, she was like some circus juggler keeping all the balls in the air at the same time.

A Little Recreation

Business was always brisk in the local pub, with a lot of money changing hands. Deals of all sorts between farmers from all over the parish took place most weekends with or without a bit of music. It provided a place for a well-earned break from their busy lives at the end of a long week. Madge and Bernard also looked forward to going down to their friends Johnny and Rose's pub on a Saturday night for an hour or so, after a long week. Even after bedtime it didn't stop, the knock on the door, sometimes way after closing time, with people looking for baby food, bread, milk.

It almost felt like getting out of jail on a Saturday night. Bernard looked forward to meeting up with some of the local men to have a few pints and to relax for a while. He would be dragged into all the farming news, about the prices of the livestock and what they were getting at the market. He learned a lot there about farming as he didn't come from farming stock. His people had run a clothes and grocery store.

When Bernard and Madge married, they bought a large premises in Kilton, a scenic village with plenty of business to be had from all around the parish. Bernard's knowledge of how to buy and sell stood him in great stead, and he could run a very successful business.

Madge usually met up with Rose, that is if Rose could take a few minutes away from the bar counter. Bronwyn would arrive at the same time and the three friends caught up on local gossip, and there was plenty of that around. They would talk over a glass of sherry or a milk stout in the snug.

The Talk of the Parish

Bronwyn was worried about one of the local women, Kitty. She was treating her for beatings at the hands of her husband by giving her ointment to help heal and cover up the bruising. But the nurse's hands were tied. Bronwyn tried to get her to report Jerry to the local sergeant, Michael, but each time Kitty would say she just couldn't do that to the children's father and they would be the talk of the village and beyond.

'Don't you know,' said Bronwyn to her friends, 'everybody is talking about the family. The people who are concerned for them only want to help in some way. Then you have other nosey parkers who couldn't care less, and the ones who are always happy when other people have hardship in their lives. These gossips seem to thrive on it.'

Madge and Rose nodded their heads in agreement.

CHAPTER SIX

Her Perfect Choice

Lorraine Mulrennan was the local librarian and ran the library in Michelin Street. Every morning Lorraine would open the library doors wide to get rid of the dusty smell of old books. It meant she wouldn't have to put up with people sneezing, coughing and making an awful racket. It would be calm and peaceful from ten in the morning to five in the evening, Monday to Friday, with a half day on Saturday. For an hour on Saturdays, she would allow children in, under Emily's supervision.

Lorraine closed the library door behind her. She looked forward to the weekend, where she would be spending time helping her sister, Elizabeth, and her brother-in-law on the farm. She loved working with all the animals and found the farm a place of pure peace and tranquillity. She also looked forward to helping to mind her young nephew, Mickey. And maybe she just might catch a glimpse of John, one of the local farmers in his mid-fifties, and not a bad looking man at all. She knew that she was far too young for the likes of him, but thought that sometimes marriages with a large age-gap worked. John ran a large farm a couple of miles away, not too far from Paddy Reynolds and her sister Elizabeth's farm. Maybe, just maybe!

A Thorn in Everyone's Side

Maggie Pine and Peggy Hendrik looked more like twins. They wore the same aprons and scarfs all the time. They never looked clean, with cigarettes hanging out of their mouths. They talked about everyone, including Lorraine's name and how it wasn't normal. It was rather an odd name, they said, and they wondered why she wasn't called Mary or Anne, good decent names. But, of course, her mother was a 'dizzy bit of a wan', who had travelled around France in her younger years.

'God knows what she got up to!' they'd say. 'There was a lot of talk about the time that she got tied up with some auld artist over there. Sure, she never worked a day in her life, plenty of money and didn't know what to spend it on. You can image what she did spend it on! Miss High and Mighty! As they say, there's no smoke without fire!'

These nosey parkers never knew just how ignorant they were, and would never understand Lorraine. They had wicked minds, and never gave a compliment to anybody. Bernard said they were two auld bitches who should never be trusted.

Lorraine had gone to university in Dublin after all, studying English, French and Italian. Her ambition was to become a librarian. There wasn't a book out there that she didn't know something about. Anyone who loved reading was always impressed at how much knowledge Lorraine had. She was delighted with any help she could give to the locals in their parish library.

CHAPTER SEVEN

The Main Woman in the Parish

Bronwyn Redmond had grey eyes, wavy brown hair and carried a bit of weight. Try as she might she just couldn't lose it. Being the local nurse, she was up and down the county every day making house calls, while also working part-time in the local asylum. She often thought the old place very dull with its dark brown and blue paint on the walls. It definitely wasn't a homely place at all, not by a long shot. Bronwyn felt sorry for the poor little souls in St Veronica's Asylum, some of the patients having spent most of their lives in that big grey building. She often wondered about the circumstances that had brought those poor souls to this godforsaken place. The patients were broken people who might never be fixed, just left there by members of their own family, and some with no family at all. Most of the patients were a bit 'soft in the head', she had been told. Whenever she was in the asylum, these lost souls would gather around her like children looking for sweets and calling her mammy. Bronwyn felt the pressure and stress of the job, thinking that if she heard herself being called mammy one more time she would explode. She had never married or had children of her own, though she delivered most of the young generation around here and beyond.

Bronwyn just loved her job, which she saw as being about fixing people. From when she had been a young teenager, she knew she was going to be a nurse. There were always going to be ups and downs. She comforted people in their loss and smiled with people in their happiness. It came naturally to her. Everyday had a beginning and an end, and life just continued.

She had been brought up by her mother and her grandmother. Her father died of leukaemia when he was young, so it was up to the two women to do the rearing. Bronwyn's mother always praised her kind nature, and how patient she was. She felt that she had had a good start to life, and was very fortunate to have come from such a loving family. Her mother kept everything going. Rearing her children alone was hard enough, even if her husband left the family financially comfortable. Bronwyn took ownership of the many youngsters, quite ready to take them down a peg or two if they got too big for their boots, or if she saw anything out of order, like a couple of youngsters having a pram race down the road with the baby still in the pram.

One Monday evening, Bronwyn was making her way over to Madge's shop when she heard a frightful fuss down the road. Off she went to investigate. One of the young children had fallen out of the pram and the young girl promptly picked up the baby and dusted down the child like he was a toy and put him back in the pram. Bronwyn was angry with the youngsters at the mother's putting the children in such danger. She first checked the baby to make sure the child was alright, then warned the children that if they ever did such a thing again they would be brought straight to the barracks and the guards would deal with them. Bronwyn hoped that a threat of the guards would sort out this type of behaviour. Bronwyn often wondered if Matthew had fallen out of the pram too. He appeared to be at least a couple of years behind other children his own age.

She always felt she had the authority to step in and sort the children out, if the parents weren't around or interested. Some of the locals had large families and were usually glad of any kind of help, even for an hour or so. The young girls seemed happy enough to wheel the babies around for a while or take them for a long walk. The parents never saw any danger. The community was tight-knit and almost everybody gave a helping hand where they could. But Bronwyn didn't believe everyone was like that. There were mean people around who wouldn't walk the length of themselves to help anyone, and she had a few mean-spirited people in mind when she thought this, that was for sure.

She was exhausted after spending most of the night up with one of her patients who lived up on the mountain and was dying of throat cancer. She wondered how Bridie had developed that type of cancer considering she or her husband Jimmy never smoked, though she knew smoke from others' cigarettes or pipe tobacco could do damage. She herself never smoked and her house was smoke-free. If she was around someone who smoked, she usually felt a sore throat coming on and her eyes streamed. In most cases the smokers always seemed to be coughing, though never the film stars in the pictures from America. They always looked so glamorous while smoking.

A Well-Deserved Breakfast

The smell of bacon and sausages, with piping hot tea and toast, warmed Bronwyn's heart: a well-deserved breakfast for a hard-working nurse. She couldn't get a cup of tea down quick enough. She had a splitting headache, which she knew was down to pure fatigue after working all through the night. Finally, she settled down for a couple of hours sleep.

Nelly did the cooking and cleaning for Bronwyn. She made sure after a night on duty, with the likes of Bridie, or with a new baby, or whatever else was going on, that there would always be a breakfast ready for Bronwyn when she came home.

Sarah Beaver, a young nurse who worked with Bronwyn, wondered how it was possible for Bronwyn to know everything. Sarah was only trailing behind Bronwyn, or so everyone said. The locals still treated her like a young one, even though she was nearly twenty-five years old.

Not What We Expected

Bronwyn woke up to a gentle rap on her bedroom door. Was it that time already? She was still feeling very groggy. Sarah was all in a fluster.

'Noel and Emily's mother sent for you, Bronwyn,' she shouted. 'Emily is in labour!'

Sarah knew she could have managed, but the family insisted that Bronwyn be called in. After a quick shower, Bronwyn was awake and ready to go.

Noel was in a state of panic when Bronwyn arrived. Emily was quite calm. She knew she had to get through this and there was no going back. She wasn't in too much pain now, and she knew everything was ready. Bronwyn spent the best part of three hours with Emily. She told Noel that everything was going well. He did enough panicking for everybody, marching up and down the kitchen.

'Oh, my God! How long more? Will Emily and the child be all right?' he asked. 'Are there any complications, Bronwyn?'

It was at that moment that he knew he would die if anything happened to his Emily and child. He wished with every fibre of his body that he could do something for them.

Noel's friend Jack arrived from beyond Monomer, and told him stories about what some of the rogues were up to, thinking this would take his mind off all the commotion upstairs. Emily's parents, Madge and Noel's mother were in the kitchen making the tea and coffee. There were endless cups being poured for what seemed a very long time. Young Myles was helping on the farm for a few hours.

At last the baby was born, a baby girl. Emily's father told Noel to put away the tea and that it was time for all in the house to have a glass of something: a sherry for the women and whiskey for the men. Noel and Jack had a whiskey. It was so exciting. Noel thought to himself, I'm a father! A wave of emotion swept over him and for a moment he felt panic. He wondered if he would be a good enough father to his little precious bundle.

Emily was so relieved and happy it was over. She had had a hard-enough time of it according to Bronwyn, but all was well in the end. It suddenly dawned on the new mother that she was supposed to have a boy and only had boys' names picked out. A wave of mixed emotions swept over her. She knew that Noel had been hoping for a little chap too, though he had never said it. It had come up in conversations when the lads on the farm would be teasing him about how they were looking forward to another pair of helping hands.

Emily felt guilty at having these feelings as she held her lovely baby girl. She reminded herself how blessed they both were to have such a healthy little thing. What more could you ask for? Hopefully she would have a son in the future. For now, she would embrace her new daughter.

'Noel, what do you think of the name Bronagh?' asked Emily.
The minute Noel heard the name he liked it so much that it was settled. Bronagh Emily it was going to be, and neither grandmother minded their names weren't chosen.

CHAPTER EIGHT

The Sacrifice

Siobhan and James McGrath were looking forward to getting good jobs in London. It was going to be an exciting time. They would be able to send money home to help the parents. Hopefully their mum and dad could buy a few treats for themselves. Bridie and Jimmy were parents of two children, young adults now, and had moved over to England to find good jobs. There was nothing going in a little place like Kilton or beyond.

They were very fortunate to have found well-paid jobs there within a week, and both brother and sister rented out a house not far from Siobhan's work. Their father, Jimmy, worked with the electricity supply board. His job involved setting up power lines over the mountain. His son James, an electrician also, whom he missed very much, had to make the move over to England to work for a couple of years, with no jobs at home at the time. Now with electricity going all over Ireland, there was plenty of work and Jimmy hoped that James would come back home soon.

Siobhan worked in a big department store in the heart of London and was making very good money. She was very fortunate to have gotten a place in the National College of Art and Design, and her parents were only too happy to make the sacrifice to get her through. Now it had paid off. Her job included advising people on how to dress for special occasions. She had an excellent eye for style. Her boss, the owner of King's department store, Mr Raymond King, would often say that about Siobhan. He couldn't fault her at all, as he stood in the wings of his store quietly admiring her work. In fact, he had told one of the top people in his department store of how fortunate he was to have hired her. He went on to say what a big asset she was to the business and that people like Siobhan rarely come along, with her sunny nature, always smiling and ready to help the customer. Raymond also knew that he was falling in love with this Irish girl, this raven-haired beauty, and he didn't know what he was going to do about it.

Jimmy kept a couple of cows on a bit of land he had bought before he married. He later built a small thatched cottage on the land when he met his wife Bridie. Siobhan could smell her mother's baking, when remembering those precious memories from her childhood years. She missed her family, her friends and her best friend Emily. But she would only remain in London for a while longer. She would have a decent amount of money put by soon and would be able to come home, and maybe get a good job somewhere in Ireland. Siobhan believed she would get the chance to put into practice all that she has learned in London and maybe even become one of the main buyers for one of the top stores back in Dublin or Cork. That was, until she decided to buy her own premises when the time was right.

The Right Place at the Right Time

Siobhan had been waiting for the right opportunity to buy her own fashion house. She felt confident and that the time for dreaming was over. She could be back home with no ties to hold her in London. It was a good place if you weren't afraid of hard work. She knew how fortunate she was to be given such an opportunity and to work with masters of fashion and design in such beautiful surroundings. The top designers came over there from France and Italy. She still could hardly believe her luck. Or maybe it had been all those prayers and candles, her parents praying for her and James every night. One way or another she was delighted at how everything was working out for her. It would have been impossible to get an opportunity like this back home. It was the chance of a lifetime.

Siobhan missed her mother a lot. Being the only girl, they were always very close. She hadn't really wanted to go away, but with no money of her own she couldn't live off her parents forever. Hadn't they given her an education, which they said was a ticket to life? With it, she could travel the world.

When she and her brother James had headed off to London, the parents job was done and it was time to let them go. Jimmy told Bridie that their children would have a better life, as both parents wiped the tears from their eyes.

Grief

Bronwyn wondered why their father hadn't told Siobhan and James how ill their mother really was. Bronwyn had spoken to Siobhan on the telephone and explained why she hadn't been in touch earlier. The truth of the matter was that their father wouldn't allow her to tell them. He didn't want to worry them until the time had come when he had no choice but to let them know.

Emily wrote to Siobhan at least once a fortnight, filling her in on all the news. She suggested that maybe it was time for Siobhan to come back home. People were getting jobs, again she told her, and there was plenty of money floating around once more.

Emily ran down the hall to answer the phone. It was Siobhan. She was sobbing and Emily couldn't make out what she was saying for a moment. Siobhan told her that James and herself were coming home and would arrive by boat on Friday. Emily heard that Bridie wasn't well, but she hadn't realised how sick she really was. She was mad at herself for not calling to the house just to keep in touch. With the baby and everything else, life just had a way of galloping by.

The Loneliest Feeling in the World

Jimmy Mc Grath was all alone. With Bridie gone, the silence in his home was almost unbearable. He rubbed away his tears and with a broken heart, he remembered with great sadness a time that had been busy and full of living. He wondered where did time go. There were no more children, no more Sunday outings picking up beach pebbles or seeing all sorts of wild life in the forest. Bridie wouldn't know what kind of creepy crawlies she would find in Siobhan's or James's pockets, and always pretended to be horrified when she was washing the children's clothes. Now, instead of all the playing and squabbling that went on between the two siblings, the only sound heard in the house was from the grandfather clock, a lonely sound for Jimmy.

CHAPTER NINE

A Longed-For Adventure

Sarah longed for adventure. There was not much chance of that, with an over protective mother who was always on to her to make a good match.

'What is wrong with Dr John McCovering's son, Tom?' her mother would say to Sarah's father on occasion. 'Aren't they good friends. Isn't he a qualified dispenser now? Wouldn't he be a great catch!'

Tom and his wild college friends were in to partying in a big way. They loved plenty of drink and fun. It was not a time for settling down. There was a lot of living still to do. He kept in close touch with his friends from home and the parties continued after he graduated. The rumours were wild and the stories about Tom got bigger and more outlandish each time his name came up in conversation.

'God, but aren't some people awful for spreading terrible gossip in the locality,' said Bronwyn to Bernard when in doing her shopping.

'The local guards should fine those who take people's characters away and bring the likes of them to justice!' answered Bernard.

Tom had no intention of settling down, and Sarah, being one of his friends, felt the same. She began to feel restless with village life and longed to go to Dublin for a bit of adventure. Tom was alright as a friend. She never thought of him as marriage material. He was just a good friend who was great fun, and kept an eye out for her like she was his little sister. Sometimes he made her feel claustrophobic he was so protective of her.

Sometimes Sarah and her friends did get invited to the odd party and usually didn't get home until early the next morning, even if that meant not performing at her best in her job. Sarah remembered back to her early childhood. Even now it still made her laugh, though it was no laughing matter at the time. She was only six years old on a day in school and it had caused a ferocious fuss. All she had wanted to do was make her own sandwich and Mother Veronica got awfully cross with her. She took the knife from the kitchen drawer. She had brought in a half a loaf of brown bread and a carrot from the sack in the shed. It hadn't mattered that the carrot wasn't washed, as her mammy always said a bit of muck never killed anyone. Sure, didn't she always pick the apples up off the ground in the orchard. There was plenty of muck around and it hadn't killed any of them yet.

The Bitter with the Sweet

There was a terrible row at home. Sarah's mammy gave her daddy his dinner before telling him. He was always in good form after he ate his dinner. Sarah' mother even made his favourite pudding, apple crumble, to try and sweeten him up. She wouldn't have told him what had happened except she was sure that he would hear it from someone else. The entire school would be bringing the news home to their families, with a fair bit added on to the story for good measure. You couldn't hide anything that went on in the school. Her mother prepared herself for the uproar the news was going to cause. When she told him of what happened in the school, he blamed the Mother, then blamed Nancy the housekeeper too for not watching her!

To this day, Sarah was capable of causing a commotion. Her mother always said that her daughter was unique and no other like her. Sarah had a restless nature and couldn't help how she felt about rural life. She just couldn't settle down in her home parish and had hoped to move away soon without causing too much fuss.

Not Concentrating on the Job at Hand

Bronwyn had noticed a change in Sarah these last few months. She wasn't herself at all. When asked to do a job she could be quite short and snappy. She began to arrive at the dispensary late most mornings, with black circles under her eyes.

It all came to an abrupt end one morning when Mary Kate brought her baby in for a check-up. Sarah took the baby out of her mother's arms, brought her over to the table and laid her down. Just for a moment she forgot about the baby. She was walking to the medicine cabinet when she heard a thud, then silence, followed by an unmerciful scream. The baby had fallen off the table and hit his head badly on the floor. The colour drained from the Mary Kate's face as she began to run to her child's rescue. Sarah was snow-white and couldn't move.

Bronwyn heard the screams of the baby from the next room. She burst through the door to see what had happened.

'What in heaven's name has gotten in to you, Sarah?!' she shouted. Bronwyn calmly took over, making sure that everyone was alright. Finally, she and Sarah had to face facts: she would get the sack or get her life sorted out.

Sarah knocked on Mary Kate Raffey's door armed with a white laced mantilla for her. She also brought Mary Kate's children a big bag of sweets, with bars of butterscotch, pineapple bars, bull's eyes and Peggy's legs. Sarah was in great distress after what happened. She couldn't understand how she had taken her mind off the baby, even if it was only for a couple of seconds. She was so upset for the rest of the week that she was ordered by Bronwyn to take a few days off to get herself together.

Mary Kate said the baby was alright. Nothing was broken so not to worry. She was pleased that Sarah had come to apologise and felt there had been no need for the gifts, even though she loved her present and the children couldn't wait to get at the sweets. Still, with a heavy heart, Sarah said her goodbyes.

CHAPTER TEN

A Time of Nostalgia

Paddy O'Gorman, one of the local men in the parish and a very good friend of Bernard and Madge's, would leave the women ten parishes behind for talking. It didn't matter where he was coming from or going to, whether it was a funeral or the market fair. Paddy was affectionately known as the Baker, not that he ever did any baking.

He had been at a funeral in one of the neighbouring parishes a few weeks previously when he ran into Jack Murphy, an old sparring partner from his hurling days. Jack was surprised to see him, and turned to him, saying,

'Baker, I see you're still alive!'

'No thanks to you,' answered the Baker. 'If you had your way, you would have killed me with that hurl of yours years ago. Although I suppose it was payback for when I knocked your front teeth out!'

'You sure did, Baker. And my girlfriend Ellen was none too pleased with you!'

They had had many a laugh in the local dispensary, being stitched up side by side, never feeling the pain, or at least not showing it anyway. After the matches the lads would head off for a few pints in their local pub, Coney's, for a well-earned Guinness.

'Them were days!' said Paddy. 'They all ended way to fast.'

They both laughed, feeling nostalgic at the same time.

Excitement in the Air

Emily and Noel busied themselves, cleaning up and getting ready for the party to mark Bronagh's arrival. With no official christening party, the family would finally get the chance to wet the baby's head. Noel was whitewashing the walls in the yard, and Emily decided to give the sitting room a fresh lick of paint. She thought a nice buttermilk colour for the walls, with a coffee-coloured border would do nicely. Emily asked Noel about the rug that was on display in Weston's shop and said that they should get it if it hadn't been sold already.

Emily was in a right fluster baking up a storm. She had just finished making the tarts, rhubarb and apple the day before the party She would borrow some teapots from her aunt Madeline. Her mother baked a large fruit cake and she had the christening cake back in her house. There was to be no christening celebration in the Howard household, though they were thankful that Alice had gone to such trouble for their child. Emily had said with tears in her eyes that there would be no fighting over their child.

Emily reminded her mother not to forget to bring the cake with her. Suddenly it hit her like a ton of bricks. The blue cake! She had forgotten to buy some pink and yellow ribbons to put around the cake. Unfortunately, now it was too late, there was nothing to take that blue look off. Her heart sank. She would have to grin and bear it.

Family and friends arrived early in the afternoon. The kettles were put to boil, the ham and chicken was carved, a nice salad and homemade brown bread were prepared, so that only the cake was missing. Just then Erin arrived with the cake and called her daughter over to have a look. Alice had changed the blue icing for pink and dressed it with white rose petals. It was a sight to behold for a much-relived Emily. She kept hugging Alice and her mother. She was so sorry for her stupidity. Although she also blamed all the know-it-all mothers that had told her she was expecting a boy. She thought how she should have listened to Alice when she advised her to put a few colours in the icing.

Noel was very proud of the job he had done on cleaning up the garden, and putting a fresh lick of paint on the walls, which freshened up the house. Everything went very well.

'With all the work done maybe we should think of having another child straight away!' he teased Emily with a wink. 'Think of the fun we will have trying Em?'

She laughed and said, 'Well, you will have to settle for a big hug for now!'

'God, isn't it a grand job altogether,' said Noel to Emily, both standing back to have a look at his work. 'Life doesn't get any better than this.

He drew Emily close then gave her a long lingering kiss, not caring who was watching.

'Maybe we can teach them a thing or two,' he joked. 'What do you say about that Mrs Emily Howard?'

Though Noel had a heaviness in his heart over his father, he would never let on to Emily how bad he really felt. She had enough on her plate with the whole sorry saga. He was ashamed of his father, of his ignorance over religion. He had been half hoping his father would come over to the party. He was heartbroken for his daughter. Her grandfather did not want to recognise her, his own kin, all because her mother was not of their faith. For the life of him he couldn't understand how his father could continue this family feud, which had been going on for nearly four years.

'My mother is nearly gone mad with the situation,' he told Jack. 'Thank God for Emily's father. It was hard in the beginning, but now we have gotten used to each other and he is a real gentleman. That's why I find it so hard to understand my father's anger. God, Jack, I don't know how much longer this will carry on?'

Noel's mother arranged for Emily to call over to the house for afternoon tea with her granddaughter. Between them they would work on 'himself', the grandfather. Madge and Bronwyn were also invited. The 'boss man' came into the house for his usual mug of tea, only to find his kitchen full of women. He tipped his cap and grumbled a hello at the women, half looking over at Emily and his grandchild. Just for a moment he could feel a bond with the child. But then he remembered how she was only half a blasted Catholic and had no right to be in his house. He couldn't let feelings come into it and he imagined all the people looking at this setup, pitying him. He didn't want anyone's pity. He drank his tea out in the barn and didn't come back into the house until they had all left.

'As long as I'm alive, she or her mother won't be welcome in this house!' said he to his wife.

Jack even tried to get around him but to no avail. Noel's father answered,

'I only wished you were my son, Jack. I know you wouldn't have gone off and married a papist!'

Jack knew he wouldn't be repeating this conversation to Noel.

CHAPTER ELEVEN

The Aristocrat

Beatrice Ruth lived in Belmont Avenue and was a relative newcomer to the village. She made the move to Kilton about four or five years before in a shroud of secrecy. Everyone wondered who she was, why was she here and why had she never married, being in her late forties and still a fine-looking woman. When out shopping, people would stare at her like she was one of those big film stars from Hollywood. The local people talked amongst themselves and would say she must have come from a faraway land. They thought that no-one as beautiful could have been born and reared in Ireland.

Beatrice Ruth put away her breakfast dishes. It was a lovely July morning. She thought that she would call down to the Kavanagh house to see if Catharina could come along with her to do some shopping. Beatrice liked the young girl and they seemed to be kindred spirits they got on so well. She felt that she could talk about almost anything to her.

Catharina had also taken a liking to Miss Beatrice, as she called her, even in her own house. Catharina admired the way she dressed. She wore beautiful clothes and gorgeous red lipstick. She would allow Catharina to look at some of her gold chains, pearls and other things in her special gold box.

Mr Kavanagh, Catharina's father, was one of the local gardeners in the parish, and cut just about everyone's hedges, pruned their roses and did whatever else that needed to be done in the garden. He was known as one of the best in the parish if you were fortunate enough to get him. Madge and Bernard always praised his work, and with all the traffic that came in to their shop, it got him plenty of work in the locality. Miss Ruth praised his gardening technique and said he was a top horticulturist and Beatrice would give him a decent wage at the end of each month.

Before he finished up in the evening she would call him in to her perfect kitchen and give him a cup of tea with some fancy biscuits. Of course, John

Kavanagh thought it was very funny to be drinking tea out of a bone china cup with a saucer. He wondered what kind of a woman she was, with all that paint and powder on her face, and speaking like she had a bag of marbles in her mouth. He wasn't judging her. He felt she needed minding as she seemed vulnerable to him, with a sadness about her. There is something about her that he couldn't quite put his finger on. He told his wife Maude about the queer ways of Beatrice Ruth.

Maude Kavanagh felt a certain unease about this woman, who her daughter was always talking about. It was 'Miss Ruth this' and 'Miss Ruth that'. She even noticed her daughter had started to speak very posh. Catharina took to washing and polishing the half of the bedroom she shared with her sister Vera. Vera thought she was getting far too grand altogether. It created awful jealousy between the pair and it got so bad between the two of them with all the arguing that went on that they even started snapping at each other around the kitchen table. It was time to sort it out as it had been going on far too long, ever since Miss Beatrice Ruth started bringing Catharina shopping and on day trips to Dublin and Cork. Beatrice thought it was time well spent as she tried to instil some culture in the young girl.

Catharina's mother simply had to take matters into her own hands. Maude asked Miss Ruth if Vera could go on one of her day trips to Dublin instead of Catharina, just so that she could feel special for one day. Miss Ruth said she would love to bring Vera along but of course she would be delighted to bring Catharina as well. Maude Kavanagh felt very disappointed, but glad at the same time that her young daughter Vera was given a chance. Catharina, her mother knew, was Miss Ruth's favourite. It was obvious why poor Vera was so very jealous and it had created a major division between the two sisters.

Catharina's father liked Beatrice and was sure that she must have some sort of a story. He felt sad for her as he sensed she was living in the past. Could she have come from one of those big grand houses, he asked his wife. He wondered how she had ended up in this parish, all on her own. His wife agreed that it was all rather odd.

Beatrice indeed had a past but wouldn't talk about it to anyone, least of all the locals, some of whom were very nice, though not all of them. Beatrice had lived with her parents until the day she had been married. Her family were wealthy aristocrats who lived in a large Victorian mansion. They had never approved of Freddy Dunbar and thought he was not of their class. He was also a politician, and therefore almost never at home. What could he offer Beatrice? He came from a middle-class background, and they thought that though his family had some money, that alone could not bring class. One did not need to have money if born into the upper class and the pedigree that comes with it. 'He definitely won't fit in,' her parents said many times, but Beatrice would never listen. It was with a heavy heart that her parents agreed to the marriage.

The big day finally arrived and everything went off well. The young couple went on honeymoon to Rome and spent three weeks abroad, arriving back to their beautiful home in Dublin. All their friends could see how very much in love they were. Freddy and his new bride had bought their house in Margin's Square in Dublin. It was quite near his place of work in government buildings. Beatrice and Freddy had hired an interior designer to make over their house with beautiful colours. They were very pleased to leave everything to their interior designer; after all, he had worked in Paris and Rome, and they trusted him completely.

Having purchased rosewood and mahogany furniture for the entire house before they got married, all they had to do was walk in to their splendid home when they returned from honeymoon. As a surprise, Freddy had bought a baby grand piano and had it installed in the drawing room near some French doors. It was a sight to behold. When Beatrice walked into the room, she was speechless and gave her husband a look of pure love for being so thoughtful. She just couldn't wait to show off her home to her parents and prove what a good man she had married.

Beatrice's father and Freddy had disliked each other from the moment they met. He would never forgive Freddy for taking his daughter away from him. Beatrice's mother tried to see the good in Freddy, but if she was truly honest with herself she didn't like him either, though she couldn't quite figure out what it was about him. She wasn't a snob. She didn't mind that much that he wasn't of their class, once he made her daughter a good, kind husband.

Beatrice found it hard but tried to keep peace between her parents and her husband. She just couldn't get Freddy to let things go. Lately he seemed to take offense at everything they said and did, which wasn't at all like him. Freddy felt his parents were saints compared to his in-laws, who had to put up with Beatrice. He knew she was a kind person and would never hurt or insult them, but she just made them feel uneasy around her.

He was sorry that he married her, or at least he felt that way now and again. He really did love her, so why was he picking faults in everything she and her parents did? He hadn't realised she wasn't good at housekeeping. He had taken it for granted that this just came naturally to a woman. The help did everything in the house, but Beatrice had many more qualities that stood her in good stead and which were a help to her husband in his job.

She was very good at organising just about anything, arranging food and clothes collections for the poor, making up parcels with a mixture of toys for the little African children. Her family had always taken care of the poor and she wanted to carry on this tradition.

Freddy knew he loved her, but his feelings had changed towards her after only a couple of years of marriage. He spent most of the time in work and at his club. Freddy knew Beatrice would be a major help in his career, being a well-travelled and cultured woman. He also knew that she loved him and would do anything for him. She would allow him to have informal meetings in their home with colleagues, providing plenty of fresh food, anytime of the day or night. All Beatrice needed was a bit of notice so she could rearrange her schedule. His friends were in awe of his lovely wife. Beatrice was always roped in to help with one charity or another, much to her husband's annoyance. He felt that his wife was being taken advantage of, but she never felt that way. She had made some good friends through the experience and soon got to know who the genuine people were and were not.

A High Price to Pay

Beatrice couldn't wait to tell him the good news. Finally, they were going to become parents. She sat up and waited until he got home. It was going to be a late night, he had told Beatrice. He would be spending time with the local councillors. As soon as he walked through the door Beatrice knew he had a lot of drink taken. When she questioned him about the drink, he started to shout at her accusing her of spying on him. Before she knew it, she was on the ground. He had struck out with all his might, he was so angry. She was not at all a big woman. She was tall, but slender and carried no weight, so it wasn't surprising when she fell down so fast. He stormed out in a mad rage.

Beatrice managed to pull herself up and phone her doctor, who arrived at the house shortly after. She knew that she had miscarried and lost the baby. The doctor was just as upset for this quiet timid woman and was livid at her husband's treatment of her. The doctor had advised her to leave this man who would hit a helpless woman, this man who people depended on to run the country!

Freddy arrived back to the house at lunchtime the next day full of remorse. He loved Beatrice with all his heart, but the pressure of work was getting to him, he told her. He couldn't concentrate on his work, and didn't understand why. It was a huge blow when he learned of what happened to his wife and his unborn child.

'Oh, my God!' he cried, 'What was I thinking? How could I have been so cruel!'

He had been so full of whiskey, he had barely been able to see where he was going, never mind boxing a defenceless woman. He had never been a violent man, so what had happened to him to make him strike out at his wife?

Freddy made an appointment with his doctor to try and get to the bottom of the severe headaches he'd been having these past months. He thought that perhaps it was the eye specialist he should have made the appointment with. He would just have to wait and see.

The test results from the hospital had arrived back to the surgery. It was possible he had a brain tumour. He would have to go into hospital for more tests. The prognosis wasn't good after they discovered that he had a tumour. It seemed to be inoperable and nothing could be done about it. He was given six months at most.

Beatrice felt a knot in her stomach as the panic took hold whenever they had a meeting with the specialist, who couldn't give them any hope at all, as both had hoped for a miracle. Beatrice tried to forgive him over the loss of her much-longed-for baby. It seemed like a dream come true when she had become pregnant. She wondered if everything now was really happening and thought, please, someone take me out of this nightmare.

Beatrice went to her parent's home and told them that Freddy was dying, with only a few days left to live. The hospital rang her parent's home asking her would she please come back up to see him. They told Beatrice that he was asking for her all of the time.

'I'm still his wife,' she told her parents, 'I must go to the hospital.'

With good memories and the love she still had for Freddy, she made her way to her husband's sick room. He was in a coma when she arrived at his bedside. The doctor told her that he could probably hear her if she wanted to speak to him. She told him that she still felt the same about him now as when she first fell in love with him. She forgave him for the loss of their child and understood that it was the brain tumour that had changed him so drastically. Every now and then in the last while, she had glimpsed the old Freddy and the love in his eyes. She had no doubt whatsoever that he still loved her, and holding his hand she stayed with him until the very end.

Her parents came to the hospital room just in time for his last moments. Beatrice's father took Freddy's hand and said how sorry he was for the way things had turned out and that he couldn't let him go to meet his maker without letting him know that he forgave him. Then they left the room to let their daughter say her final goodbye.

A Time of Unbearable Pain

Beatrice went back home to her parent's house. Her mother fussed over her. She would look at her beautiful daughter and could see she had been through something terrible. She was far too thin and was fading away before their very eyes. Beatrice had heard her father crying in the library on his own. She wondered if she should go to see what the problem was. He might think she was prying, she knew, but she went in to comfort him. Through his tears, he said, 'I'm your father and you are my only child, and I couldn't protect or mind you.'

Beatrice never went back to live in her old home, except to organise the sale of the house and whatever furniture that was to be sold. One piece of furniture she could never have parted with was her baby grand piano. It brought back precious memories of when they had been newly married. She lived with her parents until they both died and during those years the three became very close once again. It was as though Beatrice had been their child once more. Until his dying day, her father never forgot the hard time his lovely daughter had gone through, and the loss of a much-wanted child and grandchild. It left a permanent void in his heart and he always shed a tear whenever he remembered that awful time in all their lives.

A New Beginning

It was time to sell up and start a new life and move to another part of Ireland. Kilton was where Beatrice had decided to put down her roots. She had spent a while travelling around Ireland before she chose this place, far enough away from all her heartache and to make a new start. Her mother had said in times of crises, 'it is impossible to go forward if you keep looking back. You are bound to fail, so my poor daughter you must keep going and eventually the pain will cease, then you can make a new life for yourself.' Her mother said these words to her just before she died.

Beatrice wasn't looking for anyone to replace her late husband but if she did find love again, so be it. A new chapter in her life was about to start. Freddy was the love of her life, there was no question about it. She never forgot how she felt when she was with him, and had no intention of ever replacing him. But the mind and heart don't always work together. For now, she was happy with her memories.

Beatrice bought a lovely home in Kilton, which was just the right place for her. She settled in to her new surroundings. The people were very nice. Her parents had left her very well off. Freddie had also left her quite comfortable, so she didn't want for anything. With no money worries and good investments in the right stock, she could well afford a decent standard of living. But money couldn't replace what she had lost or erase that nagging pain in her heart. No amount of money or painkillers would help.

The Newcomer

Beatrice was so looking forward to a new life and, hopefully, some new friends in Kilton. Bronwyn and Madge approached this newcomer and welcomed her to their parish. They introduced themselves to Beatrice and both the women made a fuss over her, taking her in hand until she got used to everybody in the locality. At the same time, they warned her who the gossipers were, who she could trust, and the people that couldn't be trusted. But you get the likes of them everywhere, they told her. Just have your wits about you at all times. Madge gave a nervous laugh, worried at how they might have sounded to this timid little soul,

'Now, we don't want to make you uneasy Beatrice! Of course, they are some very good people in the parish, so don't be overly concerned.'

Madge and Bronwyn knew Beatrice loved being around children. It was obvious she got on so well with young Catharina. No matter whether Beatrice went from Sunday service to the local shop, children seemed to gravitate towards her.

CHAPTER TWELVE

The Monday Morning Blues

It was eight in the morning. Bernard always came down early to get every-thing ready for the day ahead. When he had achieved this, which took him about half an hour, he made his way back upstairs to sit down for breakfast with Madge. They lived over the shop. They didn't need a big house. They were as snug as they could be.

Bernard was in a state of panic. It was Monday morning. Normally noth-ing much happened at the beginning of the week. He wondered about the large bag of flour which had burst all over the potatoes and fruit. It took a few minutes for him to take in what he saw. In the name of God, he thought, what has happened here? Who the hell had broken into the shop and left this awful mess behind? Who could do such a terrible thing?

In the meantime, Madge was unaware of what had happened downstairs. She cooked a fry and made a large pot of tea, which she left simmering on the hob. She asked herself what it was she had to do next, thinking that she must be going dotty in her old age. It was the toast, she remembered. She would leave the toast until last and have it nice and hot when Bernard came back up for breakfast.

Madge had asked Beatrice if she wouldn't mind helping her to choose a nice paint and matching wallpaper for her new bathroom. Beatrice had a good eye for style. All you had to do was look at her and her own house. Madge, Rose and Bronwyn were delighted with their new friend and how well she had settled into the parish. It was to become her new home, a place she could live in for the rest of her life. The girls liked her gentle way. They could see she wouldn't ever intentionally offend anyone. She might be a bit on the posh side but that was the way she was reared. It didn't bother anyone in the locality, just those fecking begrudgers.

A large steel bath which was kept out in the shed had to be brought up-stairs once a week for Madge to have a long soak in. Bernard had a quick wash a couple of times a week. That was enough for him. Madge found it a hard task to empty the bath, and usually went about this back-breaking work by using a jug to empty it into the toilet. When it was light enough, she could lift the bath and empty the remainder of the water out. By the time she was finished, Madge was damn well ready to have another bath! Now all that was over at last. She had waited a long time for a little luxury. She was delighted with the new bathroom and her good fortune. Not many around here knew of such things. For long enough Madge had had to have a quick wash in her little white sink during the week and a bath on a Sunday afternoon.

The Stranger in the Mirror

Madge looked in the mirror. She could hardly recognise herself. It was like looking at someone she didn't know. Another person had slowly taken her place without her even realising it. She had noticed a few lines appearing on her face – well, maybe more than just a few. Her skin looked tired, not as fresh as it used to be. The auburn colour of her beautiful wavy hair was beginning to fade. She was a little upset, as she had been so proud of her lovely hair. Most women envied her still as she looked good. No one can hold back time, she thought to herself with a sigh. But it was important to look well, especially when she met so many people in the shop every day. She and her husband Bernard had a standing in the community and must make an effort at all times.

All-Out Panic

Suddenly, Madge heard Bernard shouting, bringing her back to reality. She wondered what on earth was going on down in the shop.

'Madge! Come here quick!' he shouted from the bottom of the stairs. 'Quick, the place is an awful mess! We've been robbed. They broke in the back window, so there is glass everywhere. Make sure you are wearing your shoes!'

The local sergeant, Michael O'Connor, entered the shop at half past eight. He knew just by looking at the mess it had to be down to the local lads TJ and Tommy, up to no good. Those curs were always in trouble, robbing from the farmers, fecking sacks of spuds, flour and yellow masse, then selling them on. There was always a buyer for the stolen goods and it didn't bother them where the goods came from. This time they had been looking for money but, fortunately for Bernard and Madge, they never left money in the till. It was always kept it in the safe under the floorboards and covered over with an old worn rug. The thieves had taken what they could carry, not a motor car or bicycle between them – no brains, let alone principles.

After cleaning up some of the mess in the shop, and calming Bernard down, Madge called one of the local girls to stand in for them for an hour or so. Sergeant Michael and themselves went back upstairs and had some breakfast, and a pot of tea was needed in the worst way. They discussed the break-in and what they were going to do about it.

The County Home

Bernard gave a hard knock on Tom Barden's backdoor, a door so worn and weather-beaten it clearly hadn't seen a scrap of paint since it was first hung, and that wasn't today or yesterday. There was no answer so Bernard searched around the backyard to find Tom in his shed.

'Look, Bernard, imagine that!'

'Imagine what?' asks Bernard.

'A man gave me this shed. Come over and look at how neat and tidy it is! Just look at all the balls of twine and he has them in neat rolls in the corner of the shelf. God, Bernard wasn't he a good man? If I knew who he was I would invite him over for his dinner on Christmas day. Wouldn't that be a great idea, Bernard?'

'Will we go into the kitchen Tom, and put on the kettle?' said Bernard, worried about Tom's state of mind. 'I've brought some of Madge's fruit cake, what do you think?' said Bernard.

Within minutes Tom was back to his old self again. After they had tea

Bernard made his way over to the door, and said, 'All good things must come to an end, so off to work I go. I will look in on you tomorrow.'

Bernard arrived back at the shop.

'God, Madge! What will we do about Tom?' he said, and continued to tell her the whole story. 'Maybe we should call Bronwyn in to have a look at him,' he went on. 'With him living on his own, he might have banged his head and is suffering from concussion. To think that someone left him his shed, well now that is ridiculous, don't you think Madge?'

She nodded her head in agreement, very worried about this gentle soul.

Bronwyn spent the best part of the morning with Tom Barden. After talking to him for a while she knew he wasn't right. She noticed he had his greying worn jumper on backwards with no vest underneath and it was a cold winter day. His shoes were on the wrong feet. But these things alone didn't just show that all wasn't well with Tom during the short time Bronwyn had spent with him. His eyes lit up when he walked into the shed, telling her the same story as he had told Bernard! She knew that Tom couldn't live by himself any longer and he would have to go into the County Home for his own safety.

'Bernard and Madge, you both have been very kind,' Bronwyn said to them after her visit to Tom. 'You've been keeping an eye on him, delivering his shopping every fortnight and inviting him to have dinner with you regularly. But now it is time for him to have full-time care. What a big loss he will be to the parish.'

CHAPTER THIRTEEN

Gentle Persuasion

Emily met up with Charlotte for tea. They would discuss how Margaret was getting on in school. Both thought it was time to talk to her parents as it was her last few months in primary school. They both felt it was going to be a big problem talking to Margaret's mother and father. They had seven children. TJ was one of them and usually up to no good. You just knew by the way he looked at you that there was always something else going on in that head of his. There was plenty of talk about the Gaynor's stealing from Bernard and Madge's shop, though they couldn't be sure or say for definite. Sergeant Michael just knew from past experiences that they were trouble.

Time to Grow Up

Both Kitty and Jerry sat down before the principal, who spoke about their, bright young daughter's secondary education. Margaret's father said it was the funniest thing he ever heard and told her that Margaret would go out to work in a few months' time, then there would be one less mouth less to feed. No matter how much the principal tried to plead her case, Margaret's parents wouldn't listen. The principal even promised to get help from the community to keep her in school. It wouldn't cost them a penny, but nothing made any difference to her father. She was going to make good money for him.

Emily and Charlotte were very sad about Margaret. They knew she wasn't an ignorant young girl. With all the help they had given her in her studies and in other areas of her life, she would be well-equipped when she made her way in the world.

'What have we done Charlotte?' asked Emily. 'How did we not think, if she was unfortunate enough not to go on to further education, how she would feel. We tell Margaret the world is a big place, you can travel anywhere with a good education, you can have your pick of jobs. She worked so hard for a new life and now she doesn't stand a chance! Maybe we should have left the young girl ignorant. Then she might have got on with her lot, not aware of all she was missing out on.'

The young teachers had been very good indeed to Margaret. She didn't know how she would have managed without their kindness and respect and for that she would be forever thankful.

Margaret longed to go to the secondary school, but there was no hope of that happening now. She knew for certain how much she was going to lose out. Emily and Charlotte even asked if Mother Mary, and Father Rory, would talk to her parents, but it was of no use. Her father, Jerry, just wouldn't listen. He just wished that they would shut up and go away and not be annoying him. If he had the chance he would have given them a good box in the mouth and that would shut them up and stop their meddling. Margaret's fate was sealed.

Summer Holidays

It was the last day of school, everybody was in high spirits and looking forward to the long summer holidays. Some of the children were enrolled in the local convent school this coming September. But that was long, long time away or so it seemed to the excited youngsters. Some were fortunate enough to be sent off to boarding school for their secondary education. But God help the poor unfortunates that were going out to work in the local houses or hospitals. Others would be heading off to Dublin or Cork to work as maids in boarding schools or hotels. For it was going to be the start of a big adventure.

Margaret mulled over her fate. She wondered if she was destined to change nappies, scrub floors and take care of children? And she not even an adult. Though Margaret had only turned thirteen, she seemed much older for her years. She had had to grow up fast in the Gaynor household, hiding all the little ones from beatings, including the many hidings she got when she stood up for her mother and the little children every time her father came home from work in a bad humour.

Margaret had a heavy heart but she could also see a silver lining. She was fortunate to get a job working in the local asylum. The hours were long, and the matron at the hospital was very cross all the time. She wasn't allowed to have any tea or bread until nine thirty in the morning after starting work at six thirty, polishing down six flights of stairs before her breakfast. One of the kitchen maids would slip her a small mug of tea, but told her to make sure the matron didn't catch her with it. She finished around eight o'clock every night after tea. But the plus side was that she had all her meals at work and the food was a good bit better than at home. She was so exhausted every evening she fell into bed the minute she came home.

From Young Girl to Woman

Margaret called to Emily's house. She didn't know what to do. Emily had taught her the facts of life, so she understood how her body worked. But Margaret was in an awful state. She tore up an old nightdress and cut it into small pieces, which she folded up neatly and put inside her knickers to stop the blood from running down her legs. Emily brought her straight to the bathroom and poured a large jug of hot water in the wash basin. She told Margaret to give herself a good wash and that she would give her a towel and facecloth of her own, and also new knickers and sanitary towels. She explained how she must wear little cloth belt under your knickers to hold the towel in place and that she must keep a pack of these in the back of the wardrobe and make sure the children didn't get hold of them.

'Keep them in this bag,' she went on, 'and every time you change the little white towel wrap it up in a piece of paper and give it to your mother. She will burn them in the fire. Don't be embarrassed. You are turning into a young woman and it's nothing to be afraid of, Margaret.'

Emily patted her on the shoulder.

Margaret came out of the bathroom pale and shaken.

'Look what I have here,' said Emily as she handed her a big mug of chocolate. 'Nothing like a warm drink to make you feel better and a few chocolate gold-grain biscuits to go with it.'

Young Margaret started to cry at such kindness and thought to herself that she would never be able to pay Emily back, as she settled down to drink her chocolate and biscuits. She still felt like the young girl she once was.

Emily with a Heavy Heart

Noel came in to the house after his day's work to find Emily quite upset over the young girl. She wasn't just any girl. She was Margaret, her very special pupil! Her eyes brimmed with tears. She felt she had let her down.

Emily made her way down to Madge's shop after lunch the next day. She just needed to talk and Emily was so close to Madge, she could talk to her about whatever was on her mind. Young Margaret was very much in her thoughts and what on earth could be done about her situation. Madge had no answers. She told Emily to come in to the kitchen and sit down, then Madge proceeded to put the kettle on for a disheartened soul.

A Household Stricken with Fear

Everything was easier if Jerry was in good form. Most of the time Kitty was afraid of him, especially after a feed of drink. He would order her into the bedroom and get what was owing to him.

'Wasn't that what Fr O'Rourke said when we got married,' Jerry would say, 'go on now and we want to see a house full of children. Mind that good man of yours, do you hear me now, Kitty?!'

Kitty was horrified to this day by the priest having said that to a young girl who hadn't had a clue of what he meant. He seemed to have known more about sex then he ought to have, and him a priest. She wondered if such thinking was a mortal sin. But she couldn't help wondering if he'd had a woman hidden away to get what was due to him too. Jerry would say that sex and a hot dinner was every man's due after a hard day's work. Though Jerry didn't demand it every night, usually it was when he was drunk.

Kitty never let anyone know her thinking and tried to put things safely at the back of her mind. She shed many tears years later when she understood that she was being raped by her husband. But she had been trying to be the good wife like the priest told her to be. She or Jerry had no understanding of what marriage was about. When he came in home from one job or another in bad form, his dinner often hit the ceiling with rage. Kitty would tell the children not to make a sound. The older ones would pretend to be asleep and the younger ones would hide under the beds afraid for their lives, always feeling hot and clammy, their little hearts pounding in their chests. The youngest usually got sick and would say sorry to mammy for dirtying their nightdress again.

CHAPTER FOURTEEN

The Handsome Wealthy Bachelor

Oliver Nugent from Ballycash walked briskly into Madge's shop. He was in a panic, looking for a place to hide for just a couple of minutes. He was hoping Peggy didn't see him. He was worn out ducking and diving every time he spotted her. Madge, curious by now, asked, 'what ails ya, Oliver?' She wanted to know what was going on. In a fluster, he told her that Peggy Pine or, as he called her, Nanny Goat Pine, with her high-pitched voice, had her eye set on him. She was looking for a husband, a man of means. He couldn't blame her for that, after all he had a fine mare, a couple of auld asses and sixty acres or more give or take a couple.

Oliver was thinking to himself, having lived on his own for so long, that he wouldn't be able to put up with a woman bossing him around. He stood up tall and looked straight at Madge, admitting he would be a fine catch with his good looks and charm and a full head of hair. It was no wonder the women were after him, he said, but Nanny Goat Pine? No thanks. He went on to say how he could do a lot better than that auld gossip. If he was looking for a 'wan' to settle down with, she would have to be a fine thing with a bit of money of her own. He had no intention of parting with any of his. After all he was in the fine position of being able to pick and choose. Madge was quite amused at his self-importance.

Peggy caught a glance of Oliver from over beyond the library. She couldn't be sure if it was Oliver with that blasted sun half blinding her but just to make sure she would go over to Madge's for some fresh fish and have a look herself. Madge tipped Oliver off as Peggy approached the shop. Lightning would be nothing on how fast Oliver ran right out the back door. The sweat was dripping down his forehead. He tried to calm down and not let his imagination run away with him. As soon as he could, he would make his way back home, as fast as possible, and stop worrying about a silly little thing like this.

Peggy changed her mind about buying the fish from Madge. She went around the back of Madge's and Bernard's shop. She thought to herself that there might be a much bigger fish – maybe even a salmon – to catch out here. Bernard and Madge hadn't laughed so heartily in a long time. They put on the kettle for a pot of tea and piece of cake. Yes, sweet justice for a very important person indeed.

The Disturbance

Noel's father and mother were called down to Kerry because his father's brother was very ill. His family didn't know if he would pull through after this latest bout of sickness. Noel's mother asked if he could organise some help on the farm and if he wouldn't mind staying there till they came back home. His father still wouldn't recognise his daughter-in-law or his grand-child, which was very hard on both households.

Emily and Noel were woken up with their sheepdog barking. They wondered what was going on outside. Noel jumped out of bed, pulled on his trousers and grabbed the double-barrelled shotgun. He took the torch from the hall press and made his way down to the field. The sheep and lambs were all over the place and some of them were missing. He couldn't swear to it but he couldn't have a good look until day break. He heard a truck down the field revving up and he could hear men shouting. Noel ran down along the ditch, turning off his torch. There was no mistake. He would recognise those voices anywhere. It was Jerry and TJ Gaynor. He couldn't quite make out the others. He knew he had to get the number of the truck. Before he could turn on the torch again, he dropped it. He couldn't see anything as they drove off, taking lumps of earth out of the field with them.

Noel could see smoke coming from the shed that held the bales of hay and his green jeep was in a blaze. Emily's father and neighbours arrived over and helped put out the fire out. They hadn't been able to save the jeep. Emily made the tea for the men when they came in into the house. Both went back to bed after the men went home, but neither of them got much sleep the rest of the night.

Morning came and Noel set about searching the fields to see how many sheep and lambs were taken. At least nineteen sheep and fifteen lambs were gone. The shed looked bad in the morning light. Noel went down to the local barracks to report his livestock stolen and that the shed and jeep had been destroyed. He also explained to Michael that he marked his sheep and lambs with a yellow marker, so if they were stolen they would find it hard to spot the markings on the animals. He didn't use the red stamp that most of the farmer use. The culprits would be thinking that they were home and dry, with no red markings to be seen. Jerry would be thinking to himself that he had had a good night's work indeed.

CHAPTER FIFTEEN

No Interest

Elizabeth spoke to her friends Madge and Bronwyn about her sister Lorraine, who was in her early thirties with no sign of a man.

'I suppose she has time on her side,' said Bronwyn. 'I wouldn't worry at all. She is very pretty with that lovely blond bob haircut and blue grey eyes. And she is lovely and petite.'

She seemed to be caught up in her books most of the time, Elizabeth told her sister, and not much interested in socialising. Elizabeth felt she needed a hobby and maybe a good match.

'Time won't always be on her side,' agreed Madge and Bronwyn.

Elizabeth hadn't realised that Lorraine had her mind made up on the kind of a man she wanted to settle down with. In the meantime, she certainly wasn't going to be a wallflower at the tea and brack dance on a Saturday night, as if she was desperate.

She might consider the likes of John Cafferty, a farmer living near her sister and her brother-in-law. He always gave her a wave and a smile. He was a wealthy farmer and not a woman in sight.

Lorraine Mulrennan knew he wasn't short of a bob, driving that lovely new jeep and plenty of new machinery in his farmyard. Or Ross McKowen, a local teacher, was always giving her that wink, much as it annoyed her. He was a fine, dark-haired young man who any woman would admire. But not Lorraine, who he felt she was way above his winking, though he has a good way about him. They both went out for tea every now and again to the local hotel. Lorraine wouldn't dream of making herself too available. She had other things going on in her life. She would let him think she had anyway. Ross kept her mind stimulated with discussions on everyday matters, anything to do with how people lived and worked in other countries. They also spoke about her job. As she was a librarian, she felt she could well match him intellectually on whatever the topic.

Ross had an idea of the type of girl he wanted to settle down with. She would have to be a woman of substance and of some means. Lorraine's family were not short of money. Plenty was spent on her going to university and all her travels. She was a woman of the world, he was sure, driving a lovely new motor car, with a standing in the parish. With a match like that he could hold his head up high.

On the other hand, there was Ellen Moynihan, one of Emily Howard's best friends. Ellen was a beautiful girl with long brown hair, big brown eyes and an amazing smile. She was a hardworking teacher who loved her young students and they in turn admired her greatly. But of course, she only had herself to offer and wouldn't bring much into a marriage, so that would be no use to him, no help whatsoever. Such an important decision. Of course, Ellen wouldn't have the pedigree that Lorraine's family had, what with her working-class background, her father a gardener in the local convent and mother a housekeeper for the local clergy, but Ross knew for sure that he loved her and she was the one for him.

But that was something he would have to work on because he would have to ignore those feelings for Ellen. He couldn't let sentiment come into this very important decision he had to make. After all, money was very important. If he married Ellen she would have to leave her teaching post straight away and then how could they possibly have a good standard of living? Ross knew he had been fortunate to have had a good upbringing, never in want for anything, so he couldn't possibly settle for anything less in his life. He wanted a good match in a wife but not to be always watching every penny. A few foreign holidays wouldn't go amiss for that matter. He wasn't planning on having more than two children either.

He had everything planned from matters of the heart to the everyday business of life. Sure, what was the hurry? After all none of those women were going anywhere soon. He could take his pick of the crop, he bragged to Bernard, who hoped he got what was coming to him, the gold digger that he was.

A Time of Peace

Sergeant Michael called to the Howard house to inform Noel that they had caught up with the whelps that had stolen his livestock. They had sold the sheep to Grant's, the butcher's over in Ballaborne, and to Mernagh's, the big farmers down in Ballywhite. The sergeant had put out a warning that whoever bought the stolen stock would do jail time too. He set about putting a watch on the movements of TJ and his father Jerry over a few days and was successful in catching all of them. This time they didn't escape the law. Michael got them to own up. They admitted to burning down the barn. The sergeant was really relieved they were not going to upset anyone for a long time. It would give everyone a break and people could get on with their working lives without having to worry about being robbed.

CHAPTER SIXTEEN

The Educators

Emily and Charlotte got in touch with Father Rory and Sister Mary, relieved for young Margaret. With her father in jail they could approach Kitty, the child's mother, once again. They would promise to educate Margaret, giving her everything she needed, including a place to study and stay. The nuns were very good and promised to give her a bed for whatever length of time that it was needed while being taught. Kitty was very glad of the help that the nuns had promised. She would allow her daughter return to school and was happy to let Margaret go to Sister Mary's convent school. Margaret was delighted that she had been given the chance of an education and a chance in a lifetime.

A New Day in the Parish

At last everything had turned around for Kitty and her children. It was to be a new start for the Gaynor family, a time of hope. Kitty's sister, Rachael, had a good job in the local hotel. She wasn't married and was prepared to move in with her sister and help rear the children. Kitty herself would be able to work a few days a week, so between them they would manage. So, it was settled Margaret would get her education and attend a secretarial course, which was promised to her when she finished school. Both teachers, Emily and Charlotte, were glad of the lucky break for Margaret, their protégée.

CHAPTER SEVENTEEN

No Ordinary Woman

Mother Rita was having a conversation with some of nuns over lunch, discussing Claire and what was to become of her when she left the convent. Claire just couldn't and wouldn't be told anything. It would be a miracle if she made it to university, even with whatever help they could give her, and making her work hard, preparing for her exams. The teachers made an extra effort with pupils who were lagging, for the convent's sake. They had to make sure their students performed well. It was important for the good name of the school.

Claire had often been told that she was one of the brightest pupils in the school, but the truth was that the nuns believed she was a know-it-all, over-confident and an under-achiever. The nuns hoped that Claire would do well for her own sake. A lot depended on it.

A Time of Uncertainty

Claire just couldn't quite keep up with all the tutorials. They were so exhausting. She struggled to stay in the university. It dawned on her slowly, how the nuns had been humouring her and her parents. She cried bitter tears after realising what they had been up to. They probably did this with most of their students and, of course, the likes of Claire who found it impossible. She felt such embarrassment at letting her parents down, never mind the convent. She felt so stupid.

The parents gave the convent very generous donations so it was in the convent's interest that the nuns got the very best out of each student. They knew Claire wasn't capable of making it in university. Oh, they'd been able to get her into third-level all right, but could she stay without them pushing her on? She was on her own now.

Claire was relieved her mother had enrolled her in the secretarial college. She could get work in the local bank, under the watchful eye of her doting father, or get work in the co-op. Claire's mother was delighted to have her only daughter back home and maybe, if they played their cards right, 'that nice man Aidan Rath', a wealthy banker, might just notice her pretty daughter.

Good Fortune for Both Parties

Claire's mother was overjoyed with the news. They hadn't had to work too hard on Aidan. He liked Claire very much. She was young and pretty. She was also glamorous in her Chanel suit, her camel and deep-green winter coats, and good-quality leather bags and shoes.

'Yes, she is the business!' Aidan would say about her, rubbing his hands together.

On top of everything else, Claire was very good at organising events in the parish. She was the full package and he was very lucky. He knew she would be a major asset to his banking career, able to give lavish dinner parties for the top clients of the bank. A match was made, a match with no regrets on either side.

CHAPTER EIGHTEEN

The Matchmaker

Sarah thought long and hard about her life. It had certainly got out of hand. It was time to embrace the future and settle down. She went down to have a talk with Rose. They went into her sitting room and, over a pot of tea, Sarah started to talk to Rose, who she had always gotten on well with. Sarah needed her advice in the worst way. She knew she was in trouble; well not trouble exactly, more like a fog that she couldn't see a way out of. She had that longing for adventure that travelling would bring. But Sarah knew in her heart the time had come to put an end to all that silliness. It was like pie in the sky, and what a big sky there was out there.

She spoke her thoughts out loud to Rose. She couldn't believe that she was about to give up on her dreams. Rose asked her, with the twinkle that appeared in her eye when up to mischief, if Madge could help and that she might have some fine single men in mind. She asked about Tom, for example, and if Sarah would consider settling down with him. Sarah said she and Tom were only friends and didn't have the marrying kind of feelings for one another.

So, the task of finding a match for Sarah began. Rose and Madge put their thinking caps on, going through the single men around the area and what they could offer a girl such as Sarah. There was John Cafferty, a wealthy farmer with plenty of money, who wasn't a bad looking man in his day and had a great sense of humour. But Madge thought that maybe he was a bit old for Sarah. There was one of the local teachers, Ross, a very handsome man who was always thinking and weighing up a situation, always seeming to have something on his mind.

'Well, yes, it might work and he's not a lot older than you, Sarah! I suppose about eight years,' said Rose. 'Oh, but wait a minute! What about Terry Rath? Sure, didn't he arrive home on a visit to his mother and father recently, hoping also to catch up with Emily and Noel. Emily and he were very close growing up, you know. Emily is more like a sister to him.'

Terry was a very successful dentist and drove a fabulous car. Rumour had it that he was looking for a nice country girl to settle down with. Terry's practice was in the centre of Cork City and was always hectic. Up to now he had spent his time chasing girls in and out of dance halls. But now he felt this was the right time to open his own practice back in his home town. His parents lived in a large Georgian house in the middle of the village. Maybe it was time to talk to his father to get some advice on such a move.

Sean McGuire, the local dentist, who was now in his seventies, was hoping to retire. There was a perfect opportunity then for Terry or Dr Terence, as his mother Claire would call him, like he had been born with a golden spoon in his mouth, never mind a silver spoon. Terence's father was the local bank manager. When he first moved to the bank in Kilton, the house was supplied by the bank for however long Aidan worked there. They stayed in the house long enough as it suited their needs well, until they were ready to buy a house of their own. He was now in a good position to borrow whatever money he needed, at a very good rate, to buy a fine house that came up for sale. Aidan, being the bank manager, saw it as a very good investment. He would have the loan paid back to the bank way before his retirement, instead of having to start look for a house when he retired.

Claire's skin was like leather from all the sun holidays and believed everyone in the parish looked up to her. The truth is she was a snob and not everyone liked her.

Rumour Has It

Rumour had it from May O'Rourke (who moved to the parish a year or so ago), that Claire had failed most of her exams, and had only lasted a couple of years in university after repeating the first year and not making it through to the second. May attended the same university at the same time as Claire. She was a gossip and couldn't be trusted. No matter what anybody else thought of Claire, some of the local people with principles stood up for her, ignoring this kind of gossip, and from a blow-in!

Madge was spitting mad when Bernard came back from one of his deliveries. She repeated word for word what May had said.

'We'll have to watch out for that one!' she said. 'Another bloody pain we have to put up with in the parish.'

She won't be invited into their group of friends. She was a woman to be kept at a distance. Madge never let her know what she really thought of her, after all she left good money in her shop.

Bloody Nosey Parkers

'Imagine that! Being so bright and yet so stupid!' said Maggie and Peggy, who were always making fun of Claire. 'Yeah, she thinks she is somebody!' Well the truth was that she was Mrs Claire Rath, the bank manager's wife, who saw herself as a very important person in the village. Claire didn't like very many people in the locality, unless of course they had a few bob and were well-heeled. Then they'd be one of the chosen few.

Time for One's Self

Claire felt very much at home when she was on a relaxing holiday on the French Riviera or on a shopping holiday in Italy. She liked being waited on. All she had to do was to click her fingers and the waiter, Franc, would come running over to her table. This woman must be somebody, he thought, a woman of substance surely, with all that gold jewellery. Imagine wearing so much of it out on the beach, strewn over her black bathing suit.

Franc spoke to the manager of the hotel about Claire.

'Why is she is so demanding?'

'Well now Franc,' replied the manager, 'why would someone with class wear her expensive jewellery out on the beach. A woman of substance may-be, but not a woman of class. I think somebody should recommend a good finishing school to her and show her how to conduct herself. But I think even that might not work for this woman who enjoys clicking her fingers to make someone feel small. All vulgarity and no class. Do not fuss so much over this woman Franc, that is unless she is a big tipper!'

Aidan, Claire's husband, was easy-going with a lovely personality. Everyone was fond of him. Terence had his dad's personality. Some wondered how he could be so nice to Claire and her a 'dragon'. In fact, they felt sorry for Aidan, having to put up with the likes of her.

CHAPTER NINETEEN

A Time of Great Joy

Emily rang Bronwyn.

'I think it is time to go to the hospital. It won't be a home birth this time!'

Bronwyn arrived at the house and told her to put her skates on because she was well into labour. Noel grabbed his coat and hurried out to the yard, bringing the jeep around as fast as he could to the front door. His friend Jack and young Miles had offered to help his father keep an eye on the farm until he got home. The milking still had to be done. Everything was in good hands as far as Jack was concerned.

Bronagh went to stay at her granny Erin's house, so everything was in order. Finally, they were on the road to the hospital, Emily clutching her case wishing she was there already. Nurses were waiting for her and had everything prepared.

Noel sat out in the hall drinking tea. Within the hour, one of the nurses tapped him on the shoulder.

'Mr Howard, everything went well,' she told him, 'your wife is doing fine and your daughters! Yes, you are the father of twin girls!'

Noel was dumbstruck for at least a minute. When it finally sunk in, he nearly fainted. He just couldn't believe he had another two daughters and felt a huge excitement swell up in him. He couldn't wait to see his wife. It didn't matter about not having a son. He felt an overwhelming love for his new children.

He made his way in to see his Emily and told her how proud he was at having such a lovely family. He gave her a big hug and a loving kiss. Emily was relieved the birth went well. Her emotions were all over the place.

'No little chap for you Noel?' she apologised with the tears rolling down her face. Noel gave her a reassuring hug.

'Don't worry one bit, Em!' he said. 'Plenty of wellingtons and dungarees.

We'll make farmers out of them yet! They'll learn to love the land like we do.'

Noel had bought his firstborn a little gold chain with her initials engraved on the heart, and now he would do the same for his twin girls.

CHAPTER TWENTY

Not in Haste

Siobhan had been thinking for a long time about looking for the right premises to open a classy clothes shop, with beautiful garments for all occasions, with the help of her brother James and their father. Their mother would have encouraged her children and would have wanted to see them making a good start in to the world of business. Both had good business heads and if she was still with them she would be right behind them, pushing them on.

Both brother and sister finally made the decision to look at four premises. Some of them were too small. There was one that they thought might be suitable. It was very spacious.

'It might work,' Siobhan said to James about the old Thompson shop. It used to be a hive of activity in its day, where most of the farmers did their shopping. Now the Thompsons were long gone. When they had died, their farm shop died with them as there were no children to carry on the business. It had been left vacant ever since.

Brother and sister decided to put their money together and purchase the shop. Between them they had a fair amount of savings, with enough left over to do up and stock the fashion house.

Emily was on hand to give her friend advice with picking out the wallpaper and paint. Charlotte threw her tuppence-worth in, smiling and raring to go, as she arrived into the shop after a hard day teaching her young pupils. Emily had been roped in once again to teach, with one of the teachers out sick with the shingles. It couldn't have come at a worst time, trying to help her friend with her shop. Her mother and her home help Nancy were looking after the children. Emily and Noel would help with the painting. Siobhan warned the two of them that this was not going to be a slap-dash job and Emily agreed with her friend.

'I will help out with the undercoating,' said Emily. 'At least that will be out of the way. It will be a hard job scrubbing and cleaning before we get the painting done.'

'How about getting help from Ellen and Sarah?' said Siobhan. 'I'll be bringing in top quality clothes and the building must reflect the quality.'

'Gosh, it must be classy as well as fashionable,' Charlotte piped in. 'It must be amazing! We'll knock them dead,' she said with a giggle, then gave her friend a reassuring hug.

Siobhan had spent time in London going to the top warehouses. It was nothing new to her, for she was once one of the main buyers for Mr Raymond King. As always, she would take her time going through and picking out the best of garments for her spring and summer collection, whether it was for her old boss or for herself. She took great pride in doing the job well. Siobhan called into her old workplace, to see her friends, but most of all to see Raymond. Everybody was delighted to see her. It felt like she was coming home. The place didn't seem strange to her at all. Mr King made his way right across the store. He could hardly believe his eyes.

'Is it really you Siobhan?'

He couldn't understand how this girl had affected him. He had been so cut up when she had left to take care of her dying mother. Then, after her mother's death, she returned to the store to work out her notice. Those same old feelings were there, and he thought to himself that now that she was back, he had no intention of letting her go. He knew he could have had his share of girls, and did, but he was never in love before like he was with this Irish girl.

Siobhan really liked Raymond. He was such a gentleman, always opening doors for everyone, whether they had money or not. He said that all who came through his doors were important and were treated accordingly. 'From the chambermaid to royalty to the president of any country, everybody mattered,' he would say. He believed that was why his department store was so successful. He knew it was the way to achieve success.

Mr King asked Siobhan out to dinner, saying he would like to discuss some ideas he had for the store. She knew she loved him, and having dinner with him would be hard, but at the same time it would be rude to turn him down. She was also curious about what he had to say. Raymond and herself got on very well when she was working with him but she always felt uncomfortable if he was too close to her. She also felt he was way out of her league and that to expect anything more would be impossible. She has made her own plans anyway and would no longer be in Raymond King's life.

Over dinner, he asked her opinion on changes he wanted to make in his store. He asked if she would be willing to come back to London. Siobhan explained that she was in the middle of opening her own shop and that she was sorry but she wouldn't be able to help him.

Siobhan had just arrived back from London. She had a lot to think about, being so excited about her shop and so torn about her feelings for Raymond King. How could he be interested in the likes of her, a little nobody from some mountain over in Ireland?

Siobhan made sure her stock was very much in fashion. Amongst the stock, she had purchased some classy Chanel pieces, which would never date. All one needed was a long string of pearls to do Coco Chanel justice. Emily was giggling at some of the designer's clothes.

'Has no one ever told these high-fliers how to create style? Who would wear these?!' she asked.

Siobhan snatched the items out of Emily's hands, shouting, 'You'll wrinkle them!'

'Imagine having a high-class fashion-house in our parish,' said Charlotte in amazement.

Siobhan knew Charlotte and Emily hadn't moved out of the county except during their college years, never mind leaving the country. Neither had a clue about the rag trade. In their student years, they hadn't had much money, and relied on their loyal friend for her fine needlework.

Siobhan was a little more than anxious thinking of how much herself and James had put into their business venture. It simply had to succeed. Failing wasn't an option.

Sarah also gave Siobhan a hand so that all four girls set about making out the list of possible customers and invitations to the shop. They thought about who would be suitable and might have money to purchase such stylish clothes. Charlotte straight away thought of Claire Rath and said, with a snigger, 'that important banker's wife!'

'She should top the invitation list, even if she is a total pain,' said Emily.

'Remember, it's her money we are after and not her company, so grin and bear it. When I was hanging around with Terry as a youngster, she wasn't so bad really. Her bark is worse than her bite.'

'Make no mistake, we are after Claire and all of her stuffy friends! I mean their money,' said Siobhan. 'So, Charlotte, it is your job to get the addresses of these rich high fliers.'

After starting off with Mrs Claire Rath, next on the list was Mrs Madge Byrne, Mrs Rose Mythen, Mrs Elizabeth Reynolds, Miss Bronwyn Redmond and of course, Claire Rath's many friends. The girls rubbed their hands with delight, remembering Miss Susanne Forman and her lovely mother, Grace.

James had almost finished the lights on the front of the shop. He had gone to Dublin to have a look at some of the more modern up-to-date lights for the inside of the shop. He had decided to look at what kind of lights were being used in the top fashion houses as his sister had to make a big statement in hers. After purchasing top of the range lighting, he had made his way back home, hoping Siobhan would be pleased. Indeed, you only get one chance to make a good impression, and he was thinking of the people with the money. If they were happy the moment they step in to their shop, and felt comfortable, they would purchase and be back again.

Siobhan was so delighted with the changing rooms, fitted out in cream gold, with a cream chair trimmed with gold fabric, and cream doors padded on the inside with the same fabric. James finished the dressing rooms off with beautiful lights, not too bright or too soft. Siobhan was so pleased with the décor. It felt like she was back in London.

Oh, Mum! Siobhan thought, if you could just see! I miss you so much! She felt the terrible sense of loss for her mother Bridie.

Emily knew her friend was upset but wasn't sure why. She wondered had she taken on too much, if she was afraid of losing all her money if this didn't work out, or if it was someone she left behind in London. After a couple of minutes, Siobhan was back to her old self again and everyone was teasing each other in high spirits between pots of tea and biscuits.

Madge was no help at all, bringing over homemade cakes. They wondered how on earth they were going to be able to buy any of these gorgeous clothes if they couldn't fit in to any of them, and then they all teased each other over their beautiful figures, with a great sense of excitement.

Lucinda, Charlotte's cousin, was home for the weekend and met up with all four friends. She was amazed at how they had transformed the old Thompson place. She felt like she was in the most amazing candy shop with these beautiful colours all around her. She longed to be able to buy some of these lovely garments.

'We mustn't forget an invitation for Lorraine Mulrennan,' remembered Charlotte, 'her being a librarian. She mixes with a lot of people, so hopefully she will bring a friend or two. Just make sure you add a little note on the card.'

She was holding up a bunch of invitations in her hand as she made her way to the post office, whistling on the way, much to the amusement of the girls.

The Invitation

Claire walked into the hall as the post was being dropped through her letter box. Picking up a bunch of letters, one in particular caught her eye. She knew by looking at it that she was being invited to something or someplace very special because of the lovely cream and gold envelope. She thought that it had to be from a chic fashion house in Dublin. Claire's friends got together at least twice a year to stock up on their clothes for summer and winter then, after all the hardship going from shop to shop, they would go to the Erington Hotel, situated in one of the most exclusive parts of Dublin, and finish off the day with dinner and champagne.

Mr Dempsey, their driver, never minded waiting. He knew he would get a very good fare and was more than happy to oblige these wealthy ladies, and to bring them back home whenever they were ready. They usually arrived back late at night. Her husband would be up in his office working which was not at all unusual for him. He never retired until late. Claire would make a pot of coffee in her precious silver coffee pot, then they discussed the happenings of their day.

Claire decided to pull out her best china and silverware. She knew she was the only one who had been in her dining room, apart from her housekeeper of course. But what would her housekeeper be doing in her dining room only cleaning it. Her housekeeper came over the mountain every day on her bicycle. She was from a decent farming family and came highly recommended. Claire was pleasant enough to her, after all it was impossible to get honest help and someone who could keep their mouth closed about what happened in the house, even if there wasn't a lot to tell.

Her husband never raised his voice and Terence was the very same as his father. They both had a lovely gentle nature about them. Claire sat down in her peach silk dressing gown and began to pour tea into her fine bone china teacup. She spread butter and honey on her toast, then slowly opened the envelope with the beautiful invitation inside. She took a leisurely sip of tea and read who had sent it.

To say she was shocked and disgusted would be an understatement. She thought, who do they think they are? Just a couple of redneck nobodies from over the mountain! She was in such a fluster that she dropped her toast on the floor, the honey sticking to her champagne-coloured carpet.

'Well, we will see about that!' she screamed in a total rage, not giving a damn who heard her. She roared for the maid to come to the room straight away and clean up her mess.

Madge was delighted with the lovely invitation, which she knew she would receive. It was all excitement around these parts. It would be an evening of pure entertainment, that is for sure. She wondered who she would ring as she raced to the phone, thinking of what to wear at the same time. The invitation said seven o'clock. There would be canapés and champagne before the fashion show started. She thought she better have some dinner before she went over as it would be a long night, she hoped. Madge couldn't wait to see all the beautiful clothes. She remembered her lovely green dress, only worn once to a family wedding.

Madge was delighted to have a chance to wear it again. Green was one of her favourite colours. She knew the minute she wore that colour against her skin that it made a big statement. She laughed nervously at the thought of such a grand occasion in this very parish.

She also knew she wouldn't have a chance to lose some weight before the big opening. Her husband never minded if she was big or small, he loved her no matter what size she was and he believed her imagination led her to believe she was bigger than she really was. He wondered what was wrong with women, complaining all the time, never happy the way God made them.

Rose, the publican, tore open her invitation. She just couldn't wait to see what it was about. She wasn't used to receiving swanky letters like this. The only post Rose ever received were bills for the business and letters from her family over in England. It was for herself and her daughter Rebecca to go to the grand opening of Siobhan's show in her new fashion house.

Rose and her daughter Rebecca set off to Dublin to buy something special to wear for the occasion, the only place to find a couple of nice frocks. Rose advised her daughter that with her blond curls she had to wear blue.

'It's definitely your colour, Rebecca!' she said showing her a dress. 'This will be just perfect with your green brooch pinned onto the low-neck line. It will look so elegant, and still show a little bit of cleavage!'

Rose decided it had to be mauve for her, a colour that suited her well. The dress she was looking at was nice enough, but she wasn't used to dressing up for such a special occasion. Her husband Johnny would be very busy with market day. But the lads would just have to help their father out because she couldn't always be there. After all, Siobhan must think highly of the Mythens to send out such a gorgeous invitation.

Elizabeth, Lorraine's sister rang her friends, delighted.

'Did you get one as well, Rose?' she asked, teasingly, knowing very well Elizabeth would be heading the list of invitations. 'It's going to be a good auld night altogether, don't you think?'

Bronwyn was sitting down to eat her breakfast. She had just come home from working through the night. With the birth of new babies, and sick people with all kinds of ailments, her job was tough, to say the least. Pouring herself a strong cup of tea, the door knocker went. The postman was standing on the step looking a bit agitated. Bronwyn apologised to him, saying that she must ask Oliver to fix her letterbox. He was always so obliging where the ladies were concerned. Then the postman could push the post through and save her some valuable time. Of course, Bronwyn wasn't the only person in the parish with a broken letterbox but there was no need to add to his misery. Bronwyn apologised again.

She sat down again, finally getting a chance to drink her tea, when she spotted the fancy invitation. She had an idea who it was from as she opened it, holding her cup of tea at the same time, making her spill her tea all over it. Well, that's what you get trying to do the two together, she muttered to herself. After drying the invitation, she was finally able to see the gold writing. At that moment, she felt panic rise in her. What would she wear? To receive an invitation through the door made it feel special. She must ring the girls and see what they were doing in the posh frock stakes.

Elizabeth laughed as she explained that herself and her sister Lorraine already had something to wear and weren't buying anything else, for the moment at least. Madge had her dress so she was sorted. Madge still had a beautiful yellow dress which she never got a chance to wear. It had always been a bit tight for her. She had planned on slimming down and hadn't managed it. She suggested to Bronwyn that she try it on. Bronwyn said down the phone, excitedly, 'I don't mind if I do. I can't wait to call over to you later!'

Memories

Bronwyn was thinking the last time that she had been to something like this was about eight or nine years ago at a fashion show in Clancy's department store in Dublin. Her friend, Joseph O'Brien, and herself had spent a lot of time together. Both were real theatre buffs who also loved a good fashion show, always ending the night up in the Gresham Hotel afterwards, discussing the show from start to finish.

Memories came rushing back of a warm summer night when the stars seemed to be shining extra brightly. They had strolled back to the hotel after seeing *The Mikado* by Gilbert and Sullivan, a fabulous opera being held in the one of the many theatres in Dublin. It was indeed a magical night a night to remember, from the exquisite silk costumes to how much they both enjoyed the show, how well they got on, at times even finishing each other's sentences and reading each other's thought. She wondered how time had passed them both by so quickly.

London Calling

'Well, it's time for me to head off,' Joseph had said to Bronwyn, 'I've been thinking of the move to London for a long time. It would be great if you would come too, Bronwyn!'

Of course, he understood if she couldn't. He spoke casually, like it didn't matter to him either way. After all, he said, she had her life here in Ireland, though he would miss her very much. At that moment Bronwyn knew he didn't ever love her. She couldn't let him see how heartbroken she was. Bronwyn had been a good friend and companion but he never looked on her any other way than as a best friend or sister. She had understood that he would never marry her. Bronwyn had known she was in denial about Joseph, but had hoped that she was wrong and had held onto that hope for a very long time.

A New Start

Bronwyn let him go with a smile, wishing him all the luck in the world, and never letting him see how she truly felt about him. She put him out of her mind and got on with her life. That was, until now. Just thinking of him stirred up all the old emotions she thought had faded away. She acknowledged that she really had loved him very much and it had stopped her pursuing any other partner. All those wasted years, she thought, and cried bitter tears. After a couple of hours Bronwyn managed to pull herself together. She filled up the bath and poured some calming oils in. She had a relaxing soak then she put on her best dress. Who was she saving her special clothes for anyway? Now she thought was the time for living instead of saving everything for tomorrow. It was time to make big changes in her life. And so, it was at that moment that she finally let go of the man she had loved for so long.

Bronwyn wanted a man who loved her dearly and couldn't live without her. Had she left it too late? Half-hearted love just wasn't good enough for her or any other woman for that matter. Now at last she would take up Andrew's invitation for afternoon tea next Sunday over at the Country Hotel.

He had never given up on her and not a week went by without him asking her out. He was disappointed at every refusal. Bronwyn thought now was the time to have a go at trying at some kind of a life, and it couldn't all be about taking care of others. Andrew and herself got on well and for the moment she was happy to leave it at that.

Roses for Siobhan

'Where did these gorgeous yellow roses come from?' asked Emily, Sarah and Charlotte at the same time, all very curious. Taking a closer look at the card, they read,

> For a lovely Irish girl with a sunny personality, may your opening night go well! From someone who admires you with great affection, Raymond.

'Well now, who is this?' said Emily.

'We know who he is, silly,' said Charlotte to Emily, 'he is her old boss! Look at the beautiful flowers!'

All three girls looked at each other wondering about Siobhan and if something had happened between her and Mr Raymond King.

The girls set about putting the final touches to the shop, making sure everything was working, and whatever else needed to be done at the last minute before the grand opening. Everyone from the parish was fascinated, even the people who didn't get an invitation like Mary Kate. She might as well have got one, she was so excited. She would have loved to get a look at the style of the people from London and Dublin. She herself hadn't a clue, but it was exciting anyway. Everyone was looking forward to another shop opening in the village.

An Invitation for the Not-So-Worthy

Mary Kate thought that she might get a peep at some of those fancy clothes which she could never afford. Siobhan bumped into Mary Kate's husband when when she arrived home. She greeted him like he was an old friend. John usually spent time up at the house with her father discussing work. They were preparing the timber for the power lines. Both men worked for the ESB. He admired the good job Siobhan and James had done with the old Thompson shop, and knew they had put a lot of money into it. How very fortunate for Siobhan to get such a chance to go away to London and bring back all her experience, he commented to Jimmy.

Siobhan opened her bag and pulled out an invitation addressed to Mrs Mary Kate O'Rafferty. Also include on the invitation was her eldest daughter, their names written with a beautiful gold pen. She came downstairs, crossed the kitchen floor, then handed the invitation to Mary Kate's husband, John.

'This is for your wife and daughter,' she said. 'I would be delighted if they could come. I know she's always busy with the children, but maybe she could get some help for this one?'

She was looking up at him, waiting for an answer.

'I will make sure she'll go so don't give her place to anyone else now, will you? he pleaded with Siobhan. He didn't understand how invitations worked.

'Yes, herself and our daughter will go to the grand opening of this big fashion house,' he said out loud convincing himself. 'No, nothing will get in their way.'

The way home on his bicycle seemed endless. He couldn't get there quick enough to tell his wife the news. It seemed too good to be true, thinking of his precious wife and how on earth she would react. The door swung open and closed just as fast as if the devil himself was after him.

'Wait till I tell you, Mary Kate! Come here quickly!'

Mary Kate looked at her husband anxiously. He was red in the face after pedalling his bike down the mountain. He never rode the thing so fast in his life. His wife sat him down and poured him a cup of strong tea. She always had a pot brewing on the hob of her black range cooker. For a moment, she thought there was someone after him though she couldn't imagine why. Her husband was a quiet gentleman.

After getting the tea down him, he finally came out with the good news, handing her the cream and gold envelope. It was a little bit crinkled at that stage, as he had had it in the top pocket of his jacket, rolled up tightly in case he might lose it and then she wouldn't get to go at all. That would be just awful, he thought to himself, it being such an important invitation.

Mary Kate sat down and opened the envelope.

'My God! Is it true? Can this really be for me?!'

This time it was her husband's turn to calm her down. He had never seen her look so stunned, not since he proposed to her a long time ago. She was so lost for words and her emotions were all over the place. She was happy and sad at the same time. Where would she get a dress and shoes for herself and her daughter?

'Sit down now and we will have the dinner and talk about it,' suggested her husband.

Siobhan knew Mary Kate would have received her invitation by now, so she made her way over to their house and asked the two women if they would they like to come to her house and try on some evening dresses she had picked out for the two of them. She had quite a few dresses from her time working in London as she would have attended numerous fashion shows for work. She could well afford to give the dresses to Mary Kate. The one she'd chosen for Mary Kate was pink chiffon, and for her daughter, one of pale blue silk. Siobhan knew her mother would have approved. The whole family were very fond of John and Mary Kate's family. Siobhan would sort out the shoes to suit the dresses so, between herself and her friends, they can well pull it together for them. Siobhan's friends had more than a few pairs of shoes in their wardrobe for such occasions. Anything to help a soul out if needed, she thought to herself.

A Bunch of Kind-hearted Women

Beatrice heard the postman knock at her door. When she finally got there she tried not to step on her flowerpots. She had flowers and herbs all over the place, getting them ready to plant in her greenhouse. With so much to do, she never had a minute to herself and her dogs, Patch and Sooty, a very playful pair that meant the world to her. Beatrice just loved her garden and had flowers all year round. She would pick a bunch of flowers to put on her parent's grave at least once a fortnight. Beatrice would sit by the graveside on a little stool she kept in her car, only taking it out at the graveside. She would spend a lot of time talking to her parents about everything that was happening in her life. She talked as though they were sitting down beside her and always felt close to them. She never felt alone. Life kept her busy. She was always very involved in charity work.

Beatrice was making her way back over to her car when she remembered the invitation still in her handbag. She went straight back over to the graveside and told her parents about the lovely cream and gold invitation as she waved it over the grave. She had received it in the post earlier in the week. She knew if her parents were alive they would be just as excited as she was. Somehow, she knew they were listening and glad for their only child.

When she had opened the letter, she had been afraid she would tear it by mistake and was extra careful. Beatrice wondered where it came from and who would send her such an invitation. Was it a wedding invitation? It was with some surprise to find the invitation came from Siobhan McGrath, who was opening a fashion house in the parish. Always a lady for style more so than fashion! It has been a long time, she thought to herself, far too long. The last time she was invited to something as grand as this was when she lived in Dublin with her husband.

How exciting her life had been when she first moved to the city, with parties and fashion shows in the top fashion houses, places she frequented often. She rang Bronwyn to ask her about the fashion show. Bronwyn told her the story about Siobhan and James McGrath, how this invitation came about and told her not to worry, that the girls would be delighted for her to come along with them.

'Don't worry Beatrice,' said Bronwyn, 'we wouldn't have left you out. This is going to be a wonderful night!'

Beatrice was very excited at the thought of such an event about to happen in the parish. She had a sadness in her heart for her late husband, remembering how his lips would curl when he was making mock fun of his wife whenever she would ask his advice on what to wear. Whether it was casual or formal meetings, or a night on the town, she had to get it right, much to her husband's amusement. He never minded what she wore. He would tell her with a wink and a laugh that she would look good in an old sack.

Beatrice was reared with correct protocol for everything in their lives, from the minute they rose in the morning, starting with breakfast being served by the servants using family silver and only the finest bone china. Lunch was served at one o'clock sharp, and of course afternoon tea served at four when the cook made up fresh pastries, tea cakes and biscuits. Dinner was served at eight o'clock sharp. It was the way things were done and you most definitely did not or ever knock on anyone's door without an invitation. Beatrice and her family dressed for each occasion so it was a big culture shock to her when she married Freddy, who had no idea and didn't understand her way of life. Beatrice had to learn, starting from scratch. It was a time for a big change in her life, but she managed well enough with the help of her husband. Her parents had warned her, then reminded her time and again, of the major class divide.

Claire arrived at the fashion house for the grand opening with five of her friends, each clutching an invitation. They were very curious about Siobhan and her brother and to find out what had led them to open such a grand shop, considering they did not come from money or a business background. They wondered how the likes of this would go down in the parish? Claire and her friends were greeted by Emily and Siobhan who both said that they were delighted they could come and they hoped they would all enjoy the evening.

Sarah brought over a tray of canapés, followed behind by Charlotte carrying flutes of pink champagne. The women relaxed into their surroundings.

'If Claire wasn't lost for words before, she is now!' Charlotte whispered to Siobhan with delight.

Claire couldn't believe these ignorant people 'from the sticks'. When she could eventually speak, she asked her friends how the likes of them could have got the kind of money to buy this place? It had been closed for so long and let fall into an almost derelict state so it had become a real eyesore on the street. An awful lot of work went into getting this premise ready. In fact, they practically had to rebuild the whole building. Claire wondered who had backed them, making a mental note in her head. She must remember to ask her husband, after all he was the local bank manager.

Everyone that had been invited was amazed at the décor, from the expensive gold silk curtains, to the cream and gold changing rooms and the gorgeous seating area. The lighting wasn't too bright or too dim. James had got it just perfect, Emily remarked to Ellen.

An Unexpected Surprise

Susanne and her mother arrived home from shopping. It was always an exhausting job but it had to be done. It was time to make a pot of tea for herself and her mum. Just before making themselves comfortable, Susanne picked up the post from the drawing room table, after pouring out the tea and bringing in some homemade cakes from the kitchen table. She kept looking at this most unusual envelope, and wondering who or where this letter had come from. She showed it to her mother, her head in a spin.

They both pondered for quite a while before having tea and a piece of cake. Susanne wanted to savour this time as she would probably never receive such a letter like this again. She asked her mother what she thought of the gold trimming on the envelope. Her mother couldn't wait any longer.

'For goodness' sake Susanne,' she cried, 'please take us out of our misery and open the letter!'

> It is with regret we are unable to attend the opening of your
> new fashion house but my mother and myself Susanne wish
> you both every good fortune in the future.

Her mother stopped Susanne from posting their response.
'We'll find a way, if only for you Susanne. We'll surely have a suitable evening dress in the wardrobe. We can manage it. I have plenty of meetings to keep me going,' said her mother, 'so don't worry about me.'

The evening of the grand opening for the new fashion house finally arrived. Madge and Bronwyn came bustling in, with Susanne trying to keep up. Bronwyn was so used to taking charge of everyone in the parish, she felt she should be at Siobhan's side. After all, she has lost her mother to cancer.

She would take the place of Bridie, she decided, thinking that, it would have been what her mother would have wanted. She would be able to keep an eye on Claire and her fancy friends, who wouldn't know what a decent person was really like.

'All of Claire's friends are a bunch of weak stupid people with issues of their own.' Bronwyn whispered to Madge. 'Of course, decent people just don't act like snobs no matter what they have,' she continued. 'What would society do without the likes of these pillars of society, as they see themselves! Siobhan was a decent person and was never on her own, with a very caring father, a good brother, and her best friend Emily, who was more like a sister.

Rose, Elizabeth and Beatrice entered the fashion house together. Rose and Elizabeth had had a sneak peek earlier, and were still lamenting that they had never been inside a shop so grand. They were in awe of their surroundings, especially when a glass of champagne was promptly placed in their hands by Ellen, who also offered them canapés. This was like being in one of those fancy sweet shops in Dublin. Their gazes roamed around the fabulous clothes, and the beautiful colour and décor of the stunning fashion house, as another glass of champagne was handed to each of these very important guests.

Sarah, Charlotte and Emily mingled with the guests. Ellen told them to wait for her as she had no intention of being stuck with Claire and her stuffy friends. Mary Kate and her daughter were standing in a corner of the room not quite sure how to mingle. They weren't sure if they were good enough as they were lacking in confidence. They were afraid to talk to anyone.

'Sure, aren't they money people,' Mary Kate said to her daughter. 'Why would they be talking to the likes of us?'

Bronwyn came to their rescue, leading them over to the girls and giving them a flute of champagne and some canapés. They had never ever tasted food so nice and so exotic. The champagne made them feel a little floaty. Mary Kate's daughter said to her mother and to Bronwyn that she felt like a real princess.

'How lucky we are to be invited to such a posh shop for such an important occasion! Siobhan was so good to us, Mum,' she said with tears in her eyes.

She pinched herself to make sure she wasn't dreaming. Just looking at all the lovely clothes, they both were mesmerised at the sight.

After a while they relaxed a little, looking very elegant in the lovely evening gowns Siobhan had lent them, which made them fit in with everyone; that is, everyone except Claire and her snobby friends. Mary Kate did not mind at all, saying to herself that she wasn't beholden to the likes of Claire.

'Aren't your father and I great believers in only buying what we can afford,' she told her daughter, 'and if that means saving up every penny, we are happy to wait as it's much more exciting when the new table, chairs, fridge or cooker arrives after paying for the goods in full. It's very important,' she went on, 'not to owe anyone anything or borrow from anyone either. We might not have big standing in the parish, but are honest hard-working people, and an honourable family who would do a good turn for anyone in trouble, helping the sick, or cooking the odd dinner for the less well-off.'

'Move over there,' said Bronwyn, 'let's have a look at these grand clothes. But let's finish this lovely champagne first!'

Madge, Rose, Elizabeth and Beatrice promptly finished their drinks then all were ready for action.

Bronwyn brought Mary Kate and her daughter over to mix with everyone. Elizabeth, Susanne and Rose were in high spirits and of course, all 'the help', as everyone jokingly called them, meaning Siobhan's friends.

Claire's friends had started to chat with the others. Claire had just come out of the powder room, and considered how it must have cost them a small fortune on that room alone! She bumped into Ellen and Lorraine who were in great form.

Charlotte glimpsed Mary Kate coming towards her. She caught her by the arm and led her to where all the chat was going on.

'What do you think of this beautiful fashion house?' Charlotte asked Claire, dragging her in to the conversation whether she liked it or not. Claire felt like a fish out of water looking for help from her fair-weather friends, who all seemed to have deserted her.

A Moment of Panic

Claire wondered how she would get away from them but at the same time she knew she had to answer Charlotte's question.

'I have never seen the likes of this around these parts. 'It's amazing! Siobhan got it right, for sure,' said Claire.

Sarah piped up, 'So, would you agree Mary Kate?'

The ball was in Mary Kate's court. She took a moment to think of how to answer. She didn't want to sound or look silly or make a show of herself. With all the confidence she could muster, she pulled herself up to look taller and not have a hunched look about her. She always felt that taller people commanded more respect.

'Siobhan has put a lot of thought and effort into designing her fashion house, both inside and out. She has brought all her London experience back to her parish and how fortunate we all are for that. For sure, the likes of this would give the top fashion houses in Dublin or Cork a run for their money. Her family can be very proud of her wouldn't you think?' she finished, looking straight at the girls.

Claire and the girls looked over at Mary Kate with new found respect for this woman who could speak well. Her grammar wasn't bad, Claire thought to herself. She wasn't quite the ignorant woman she had believed her to be. The conversation turned to the amazing wallpaper.

'She must have brought that back from London,' said Beatrice, 'there are such wonderful fabrics available there.'

For once it was Claire's turn to feel uncomfortable. Beatrice was such an elegant lady and spoke very eloquently. Claire thought she should make the effort to get to know Beatrice and introduce her to some of her friends. It was said that she came from an aristocratic background.

Of course, Beatrice had made lovely friends of her own in Bronwyn, Elizabeth, Rose, Madge and Susanne. They all had plenty in common and were a bunch of well-respected decent women with not one gossip amongst them. Beatrice gave Mary Kate extra-special attention, and Beatrice was going to make sure she would not feel intimidated by anyone anymore. As she pulled her into the circle of her close friends, thinking how she would make her one of them, Beatrice encouraged Mary Kate to get involved with the Irish Countrywomen's Association and to join them all doing charitable work.

A Disgruntled Couple of Auld Biddies

'The grand opening!' said Peggy to Maggie, 'well, who does your wan think she is? Sure, she wouldn't give ya the time of day!' They continued their conversation as they entered Madge's shop. 'You'd swear she was somebody with that fancy car. I wonder where she got the money for such a vehicle!'

They nudged each other with a laugh. The two women didn't have a decent bone in their bodies, and not much between their ears either.

Bernard was going mad. He felt under such pressure when they were in the shop, especially with other customers there too. He hoped that they kept a tight hold of their handbags. It wasn't always possible to watch them but he was sure the pair were helping themselves to some free stock but he couldn't catch them. He would have liked to order the two of them out of the shop but Madge stopped him. She said life was difficult enough without these two causing more problems.

'Bernard, you can't accuse them of stealing until you catch them at it!' Madge warned him once again. 'Those two biddies don't miss a thing, they are so sharp and on the ball.'

'Can you imagine if they put their energies into doing good instead of bad,' said Bernard, 'and what they would be capable of doing for the community!'

The Mischief-Makers

Maggie and Peggy were as mad as hell.

'Who do they think they are?!' shouted Maggie at her friend in a rage. 'The whole damn fecking lot of them are nothing but stuck-up snobs. We'll show them!'

The women sneaked around the back of the new fashion house, glancing behind them to make sure that they weren't being watched. They were going to go after the purses and fancy bags from those rich auld cows. The coast was clear. They pulled gently at the back window hoping it wasn't locked and as luck would have it, it was open. Maggie proceeded to climb up on an old barrel with Peggy holding on to it, a fag hanging out of her mouth. But Maggie got stuck in the window and couldn't push it open any further. Maggie started shouting loud enough for the whole parish to hear.

The Surprise

Raymond King arrived in Kilton for the opening of Siobhan's fashion house. It was to be a surprise. He hadn't mentioned anything to Siobhan. Maybe he would be able to help her in promoting her new shop. Raymond was in love with this Irish girl and no other would do. He knew it was the genuine thing, definitely love. He had an ache in his heart every time he thought of this lovely Irish beauty. He wanted to keep in close contact with her. But how could he make it work between them, with her over here and him over in London?

As he approached the shop, he noticed a commotion going on around the back. The shop was situated on the corner, at an angle so you could get a good view of the back. He decided not to investigate until he found a police station. Sergeant Michael was working on a mound of summonses. He was far behind in his filing. He swung his chair around to see who needed his attention.

After Raymond told the sergeant what was happening, they both went to Siobhan's shop to catch the women out. Peggy was pulling Maggie out of the window. Her arm was scratched from trying to get at the bags. Peggy was holding at least half a dozen purses. They were caught red-handed.

Michael didn't want to disturb the party inside. He put his head inside the door and beckoned Bronwyn over, handing the stolen property over to her. So, it was up to Bronwyn to explain what had happened to Siobhan's guests, which she managed to do very well. She was used to taking charge in a crisis and had a good dependable head on her shoulders.

'Well now, ladies,' said Sergeant Michael to the two thieves. He wanted to address them like a couple of baboons, but he reminded himself that he must remain professional always and would not allow himself to do so. 'What have we here?' he continued, as he and his colleague held onto them. 'At last we've caught you pair! It's jail for the both of you. You've been a thorn in my side for a long time!'

Bronwyn called out to all the guests, tapping on her glass and saying she had an announcement to make. Everyone grew quiet, curious as to what else could she add to this perfect evening, except for Claire who continued speaking to Sarah and Ellen.

'This fashion house definitely is going to be huge success,' she said. 'If Siobhan buys the likes of these beautiful garments, we won't have to travel to Dublin, well not as often anyway!'

Claire and her friends would continue their little trips to Dublin. It was always so exciting to see what was in season in the top shops. It was a great social outing finished with numerous cups of coffee in hotels like the Gresham.

Bronwyn began to speak.

'Unfortunately, there has been a robbery. Purses and handbags were stolen from some of you. But the good news is that all have been returned. The thieves didn't get a chance to search through the bags or purses.'

Bronwyn thought it would be better to give the bad and good news at the same time so not to alarm everyone unnecessarily. She knew that the guests would be relieved after checking their bags. Everyone was happy there was no harm done. Suddenly everyone was trying to find out who the thieves were and if they were local or strangers.

'One of the thieves is in the hospital having her arm stitched,' answered Bronwyn, 'and the other is being held in the local barracks.'

What Were His Intentions?

Siobhan was very disappointed over the whole incident, which she thought had tainted the grand opening. Emily tried to comfort her.

'Just be glad that someone caught them in time and was able to call the guards! We'll make sure the likes of this never happens again.'

So, everyone settled back down and the night wasn't over yet.

The door opened. Emily thought that all the guest had arrived at this stage.

Mixed Emotions

Siobhan couldn't believe her eyes. She felt sick and excited at the same time. Here he was, standing in front of her, the man she has loved for ever. But she always believed that she never stood a chance of gaining his affections. Her old boss Raymond King. Sarah, Charlotte, Emily and Ellen took a good look at Raymond, at least six foot odd and very good looking at that.

He took only a couple of steps and he was across the room. He wasn't at all surprised at the beautiful surroundings, with the fabrics, exquisite wallpaper, the seating and the theme that ran right throughout the fashion house. She has done it again, he thought to himself. Of course, it did not surprise him. Siobhan stood in front of him, looking for his approval like she had done many times before in his shop. That she had, and in abundance.

Bronwyn knew who the thieves were but Michael asked her not to say anything until morning. She needn't have worried because by the time everyone left the party it was all over the parish and, you may bet, far beyond.

Mary Kate and her daughter strolled home slowly. They didn't want this night to end. The women arrived back to a very warm welcome from Mary Kate's husband, who had the tea brewing on the hob. He laid the table out with their best china, which was passed down from her mother. It was taken out only for special occasions.

'Well if this isn't a special occasion, I don't know what is!' said her husband.

One of their friends had made a chocolate cake for Mary Kate to have when they arrived home. With this special treat, this party was going to last a bit longer. They sat talking about everything that had happened including the scandal. They stayed up for at least a couple of hours, as there was so much to go over. It was a night they would never forget.

Beatrice, Madge, Rose and Elizabeth thanked Siobhan and Bronwyn for the lovely opening, which had gone so well. All the women told Siobhan that she could be very happy the night went down a treat, and not to worry about the break-in. With opening a new business, they assured her, she was bound to have some teething problems. Siobhan and her brother would make sure the likes of it wouldn't happen again. She couldn't let anyone see the tears in her eyes. She wasn't sure whether it was over the break-in or over Raymond taking the trouble to come all this distance just to see her.

The next morning, Raymond asked Siobhan to join him for some breakfast in the local hotel. He congratulated her on the great success of her opening night and told her how right she got the decor of her shop. He was glad that he happened on those thieves just at the right time. Siobhan felt a shudder going down her back.

'Thank God you were there!' she said.

After breakfast, it was time for Raymond to get a taxi back to the airport. He wished her well and took her hand.

'Until we meet again,' he sighed and, with a very heavy heart, gave her a kiss on the cheek.

After he had left, Siobhan made her way over to Emily's house. She knocked on the door. When her friend answered, she took one look at Siobhan and knew she was upset. She burst into tears and Emily tried to comfort her.

'Don't let those two biddies get to you. The night was a great success for everybody.'

But they weren't tears shed for the robbery, they were tears for Raymond.

Noel popped home for some equipment. He knew something was wrong with Siobhan. He made a pot of tea for the two friends and went up to the farm again.

Siobhan told Emily that she was in love with Raymond but there was nothing she could do about it, as he was a wealthy store-owner in London. What hope had she? After a good cry, it was time to get back in to her shop and start selling clothes, a job she was very good at.

CHAPTER TWENTY-ONE

Love Came Unexpectedly

Lorraine stopped for an orange juice on the way home from work at Rose's pub, dying of thirst. It was a scorcher of a day in late May. Women wouldn't normally go into pubs without an escort, but Rose's pub was different. A woman could have a cup of tea or coffee or cold drink in the snug on an afternoon. Lorraine stood talking to Rose at the counter while she downed the orange juice. She heard a man's voice from across the room.

'I didn't think young ladies hung around pubs so early in the evening, or anytime for that matter.'

Lorraine swung around to see who was giving her a hard time. He had some cheek whoever he was. Suddenly Terence jumped up out of the chair and introduced himself. To her amazement she felt that she knew him well already. It was hard to believe they had only just met. Lorraine couldn't stay fired up with him for long. She liked him immediately, but couldn't let him know just yet. Rose watched out of the corner of her eye, quietly amused at the scene in front of her.

Lorraine and Terence spent a lot of time together during the lovely summer months, which sped by. They passed the time together on the tennis court and the local tea dances at the weekends when Terence was up from Cork. They had a lot in common and had a healthy respect for each other's views though they didn't always agree. Everyone liked Terence and Lorraine, they got on with everybody. Terence fell madly in love with Lorraine and, after a whirlwind courtship, a date was set for the wedding. Noel was delighted to be best man for Terence. They both thought they were ready to settle down and knew with all their hearts that each had made the right choice. It got harder and harder for them, with a kiss not being enough, and wanting so much more.

A Woman of Substance

Claire hummed to herself in a sun-filled kitchen. She was thinking of how well Terence had done for himself and how happy she was with the match. She thought Lorraine was one of her own, with the right pedigree, and that the wedding would be a spectacle to behold. All those priests, nuns and, of course, the very important Bishop Eamon, related to Lorraine's family. It would be a proud day indeed. Claire could hardly contain how she felt. It was a dream match. She just couldn't have wished for a better daughter-in-law. Terence was happy that both women got on so well. He knew his mother was a bit odd at times, but he didn't have to worry. It looked like they would have a bright future, settling down in a place they knew and loved so well.

CHAPTER TWENTY-TWO

A Soft Landing

Ellen became very friendly with Tom, who ran the chemist in the locality. Tom thought how lucky he was to have found such a woman. Ellen always made him laugh. Humour just came naturally to her but he could see she had a sensitive side and generous spirit as well, mindful of the wants of other people. Tom was one of the boys and loved to party. He wasn't at all short of female admirers. He had no intention of settling down for a while yet. Every time Tom met up with Ellen, he was awestruck by her captivating smile and her sense of ease. Ellen couldn't believe she was falling for Tom and wondered if she was falling in love. She knew Tom was the one for her. She was so happy to be going out with him, whether they went to the cinema or long walks a couple of evenings a week. It didn't matter where they went, she just loved spending time in his company. With him a qualified chemist and herself a teacher, they were never short of a conversation on any topic.

Ellen didn't want to rush Tom in to deciding about their relationship. She was happy the way things were for now. Maybe he needed some more time before he committed to marriage. Being in love was like sunshine in your day, only a zillion times better, Ellen thought, as she danced in her bedroom, filled with her favourite flowers, which were yellow roses.

Tom had planned to take a day off work for a very special occasion and asked Ellen if she would like a day out. Maybe they would make up a picnic, he suggested, and enjoy a lovely summer day. Ellen was delighted, thinking at the same time of what to wear. Not heels, she thought, maybe some flat court shoes and a pair of navy slacks. She would ask for Emily's advice on the matter.

She had no idea of the surprise Tom had planned for her. It was really a day trip to Dublin. On the way to Dundee Park, he took a detour, bringing her to the university where he studied chemistry. Maybe if they were lucky enough they would meet up with some of his old friends who had gotten teaching posts. Maybe it might be nice to stop off and have a spot of dinner at the Gresham Hotel on the way home, he thought. Tom loved his old place of study. There was so much reading material in those amazing old rooms, a place for your mind to get lost. Entering those rooms was like stepping into another world, one you could never tire of.

The grounds of his old haunt had beautiful gardens. Tom looked for the perfect setting to propose to Ellen. His heart began to beat fast in his chest and his hands were clammy. He wondered if this was because of the weather or was it fear of commitment or rejection? If Ellen turned him down what would he do? He was usually so confident, but this time he was terrified of what Ellen's answer might be.

She wondered about all the students that had passed through these very rooms and if they had gotten their hearts' desires? Tom gazed lovingly at her expression and how she took everything in. He could see her genuine interest in everything around her.

'My teacher training college was a big old barracks of a place,' she said to Tom, 'nothing like this at all. There is something special about this place and I'm glad for you that you got the chance of this amazing experience.'

Tom caught hold of Ellen, saying it was time for cold lemonade and chocolate cake. They went to the tea rooms across the well-manicured lawns and beside a bed of pink roses with their beautiful fragrance.

This must be the right place, thought Tom, a place that Ellen would never forget. He went down on one knee, took a tiny blue box out of the breast pocket of his green linen jacket, then dropped the ring!

'Ah no, Ellen,' he said. 'I'm so sorry!'

He began to look for the ring in the long grass and Ellen gave a nervous laugh. He found the ring then told her how much he loved her and hoped that she felt the same way about him.

'Will you do me the honour of becoming my wife?' he finished.

Well of course Ellen flung her arms around the love of her life.

'Of course, Tom!' she answered,' if you are ready, then I am more than ready to take our marriage vows.'

'The sooner the better!' said Tom, as he put the ring with grass still on it on her trembling hand.

Tom put his arms around Ellen and they made their way back over to the car. Opening the boot of the car, he pulled out a green rug and a bottle of champagne with a couple of beautiful crystal glasses wrapped in white linen napkins.

Sarah was delighted for them both. She couldn't believe that Tom was so moonstruck, that he had found his true love so soon. He told his many friends on more than a few occasions that he hadn't planned on settling down for a long time. And with a little chuckle to herself she said, 'We almost certainly cannot control the workings of the heart.'

Sarah hoped that when it was her time, the same thing would happen, but not for a long time yet. After all she had some serious living to do and wouldn't be making plans anytime soon. No marriage or babies for her for a long time! Although she had been thinking of settling down, Sarah just couldn't bring herself to give up her freedom. She had seen what marriage and children could do to a person and their relationship. Ross with his dallying got left behind and lost the two women he had in mind for the perfect wife.

CHAPTER TWENTY-THREE

Death by Misadventure

Sergeant Michael O'Connor stood outside Kitty Gaynor's house. He wasn't sure how to knock on the door, if it should be a hard knock or a soft rap. He had just come back from the prison where Jerry Gaynor was locked up for stealing from the people in the parish, even from those who were good to him. He threatened anyone who came in his way or who tried to stand up to him. He was a mean-spirited person if there ever was one, always looking for a fight.

Sergeant O'Connor got the call at three o'clock in the morning to say that Jerry Gaynor had started a fight in the cell. Unfortunately for him he picked on the wrong man, who towered over him. He had had just about enough from that Jerry Gaynor. Jerry looked mean like it was engraved on his face, and did not have any friends in jail, and that was exactly the way he wanted it. He was such a loud foul-mouthed man. It had happened so fast. Both men had been boxing it out when Jerry fell, hitting his head hard against the wall. The warden was opening the cell door when he heard the thud. It was Jerry's head, and it hit the wall so hard he died instantly. The warden heard the row and knew Jerry was at fault.

The other prisoner who shared the cell with him was so shocked he was almost hysterical. He had to be calmed down by the warden. It hadn't been his fault. He'd been reading a book but Jerry kept on jeering him about his reading, saying who did he think he was, a big professor or maybe a solicitor, or why not a judge? The prisoner didn't respond. Then Jerry came over to his bunk and pulled the book out of his hand. He tore it up in front of him, hoping to get reaction. He still didn't rise to the bait. Jerry got madder by the second and struck the first blow. It was decided by the prison governor that it had been death by misadventure.

The Dawn of a New Day

Kitty Gaynor opened the door. It was the look on the sergeant's face. She knew something had happened. He asked if he could talk to her and if there was anyone she would like to have there with her. At this stage, Sergeant Michael put his head outside the door and asked a young girl who was walking by if she could to go down to the local hotel and fetch Kitty's sister Rachael. Then he called in a next door neighbour, a good neighbour who automatically went into the kitchen and started to make a pot of strong tea, putting a mug firmly into Kitty's hand. The neighbour didn't know why she was there but knew that the main thing was that she was there at a time of need for Kitty and her family. The sergeant talked about everything and anything except the matter in hand. Kitty's mind was all over the place, as she wondered what all this was about. Was it about her husband or her son? Had something happened to one of the family over in Cattleman? She wondered how she was so calm and why she wasn't trying to get more information from Sergeant Michael. It was like it didn't matter one way or the other. The truth of the matter was she couldn't face what she was about to hear. At the same time a sickly feeling came over her like she wanted to throw up. The knot in her stomach got tighter and tighter, as she waited to be told the worst.

Rachael came in to the house, all in a fluster, racing over to her sister and putting her arms around her. They both braced themselves for what the sergeant was about to tell them. He explained what had happened in the jailhouse to Kitty. She sat down and wondered why she wasn't upset for Jerry, not even a little. Would the shock hit her later? She had had a very hard life with him. At last, she could make the best of what was left of her life with the knowledge that her children wouldn't be afraid of the beatings anymore. They had worried about what he would do to them when he had served his time in jail. Maybe now all the children could get an education and have a decent chance of making a good life for themselves.

The sergeant stood back and looked at the women. He felt so sorry for Kitty and the family of little souls, hard workers with not a bad bone in their bodies. At the same time, maybe this news might not be so bad after all. Weren't the family doing so well with this whelp out of the way? Everybody around helped the mother and children out since that fellow went to jail. Life was much better all round for this family. How do you sum up a life when there are no tears shed for them when they die, Sergeant O'Connor thought to himself and of course he knew the answer to his own question.

Kitty wouldn't be looking over her shoulder everytime the door opened. It was a relief all round ,not just for the family, but everybody from the parish and further afield. The Gaynor children were doing very well and didn't miss their father at all. They loved their auntie Rachael living with them. She was so kind and had a lot of patience, always giving each of the children a hug every day. Their mammy was very happy doing up the house, making curtains and putting down new linoleum on the floors and wallpapering and painting all the rooms. Kitty had the heart now to do up the house with what little she had, finally making it into a home. All the years of strain on her face seemed to fall away.

A year or so after Kitty had lost her husband, the sergeant called to her again. Now was the time he believed to have a talk to her about her son TJ. He was to suggest something that might suit her son very well. A large timber company up in the North was hiring workers and TJ might fit the bill, with a recommendation from them, of course. They were looking for young apprentice carpenters. The sergeant told Kitty that it would turn his life around if he was willing to go and learn a trade. Money wouldn't be plentiful until he was qualified but he would have enough to live on. Prison had taught TJ a lesson and he didn't intend to ever go back to the life he had lived before. This was a new start for a chap who knew no better. It was a new day for TJ as he returned to civilian life once again.

An Educated Young lady

Margaret Gaynor was doing extremely well in school. Her sisters were also doing well. All the children arrived every morning, clean and tidy, and with their schoolbags in order and all the homework done, much to their teacher's delight. When a challenge was presented to those dedicated group of teachers, they rose to it. Margaret had finally finished her secretarial course and was ready to take up a position in the local bank, and in turn would help in the education of her siblings. She was so thankful to her caring teachers, who hadn't let her fall through the cracks. Margaret was a very confident and competent young woman now. She couldn't look back on her young life, as it caused her great distress. In fact, it was like looking back at another child all those years ago. She often thought how different her life would be if those young teachers hadn't noticed her.

CHAPTER TWENTY-FOUR

The Blow-In

Madge and Bernard set about having a big party for their thirtieth wedding anniversary. With no children to organise such an important event it was up to them. It was so exciting. Who would come? Where would they have the party? Maybe they would have it in the local hotel as there was no room at all in their place. Not to mention everybody walking through the shop. No, Madge thought, it would have to be elsewhere, but where?

Johnny and Rose had a large hall at the back of the pub. With all those Mythens children having to be reared and educated, the pub was their only means of making a living. They could do with the business.

'I will make a few suggestions to Rose,' said Madge, 'maybe I can give her a hand with hanging up streamers and decorations. What do you think, Bernard?'

Bernard nodded in agreement.

'Madge, you always know best! Why do you think we have run such a successful business these past years!'

Madge and Bernard agreed they would be only too delighted to give their business to their friends Johnny and Rose. They could well afford the local hotel and that would be quite fancy, but friends were more important to them. So it was settled, and everybody got stuck into planning the party.

Many of the local children, of whom Madge was very fond, were always popping into the shop and gazing longingly at her biscuits boxes. She usually gave the broken biscuits to the young children. Everyone from the village and beyond knew she would have made a good mother. She always had a kind word for the adults and any young child that crossed her doorway.

Searching

One little girl stood apart from the rest and caught Madge's attention. Mary was her name. She had a head of beautiful black curly hair and the biggest dimples you ever saw. She seemed to hang around the shop that bit longer after the other children had gone home. Madge had heard that her mother had died during the birth of the child, and it had been left up to her father Frank to rear her. He was a good man, so the young child didn't want for anything, but young Mary longed to have a mammy like everyone else. She took a liking to Madge and Bernard. She was only six years old. Her father always kept a close eye on his young daughter. He got some help from a young girl who lived locally, who did some cooking and cleaning for the two of them. They only lived two doors down from Madge's shop, so it was acceptable that she spend time with Madge and Bernard. Her father knew Madge and liked her very much. He knew she would mind her well. Mary would fit in and gradually became like one of Madge and Bernard's family.

Mary would fill up the shelves and count the change for Madge most evenings. Madge would take an hour out of the shop in the evening to do homework with Mary. Of course, the tea had to be prepared first before they settled down to the hard job of doing the homework, with a promise of a little something after the hard task was accomplished.

The Anniversary Party

Mary's father asked his daughter to do a drawing for Madge and Bernard's party, but said she must keep it a secret. She set about doing what her father had asked, armed with loads of coloured pencils, her lovely curls bouncing. She thought of how she was going to do the drawing and was really happy for Meme, her special name for Madge.

Madge asked Alice to make the cake. She asked for a large fruit cake with icing on top. Half the village would have to have a slice at the party. Alice had made a lovely rich fruit cake for Rose's daughter, Rebecca's, sixteenth birthday, which melted in your mouth. Madge was also thinking of ordering at least five sponge cakes filled with raspberry jam and cream. It wasn't a time to be thinking of her weight! She seemed to be on a diet forever!

CHAPTER TWENTY-FIVE

Those Who Ponder Usually Get Left Behind

The door swung open with some force. Ross marched into his classroom, not in good form at all. He was very upset over losing Lorraine, or even Ellen! Ross thought he had plenty of time. What he hadn't realised was that the women had minds of their own, with expectations of what they wanted out of life themselves. They were fortunate enough to have made two fine matches and both girls were very happy. He most definitely missed out there. What would he do now? No one around here could match up to what he was looking for in a woman, a well-heeled woman in a good job with plenty of money a good background. Women like that were not plentiful around these parts, he thought to himself. He was more than upset. He couldn't believe this cruel twist of fate, this missed opportunity, and the mess he had made of it all.

Sarah had a good job as a nurse. She was a pretty girl, from a good family. Maybe she might come up to the mark. Ross thought long and hard about the match. He didn't love Sarah and really didn't know her that well. But he liked her and that was enough. He believed love wasn't necessary and that marriage was a business proposal. After all it was for life, and it was all about achieving a good standard of living, getting involved in the local golf club, and having standing in the community, which he believed life was all about.

CHAPTER TWENTY-SIX

A Well-Earned Night Out

Emily and Noel were looking forward to Madge and Bernard's party. They hardly had time for a social life because of their young family. Emily had a housekeeper to help. She was more like a devoted auntie who fussed over the children no end. Even so, Emily rarely ever had a moment to herself.

Noel and his father were civil to each other and ran the farm between them. Noel knew for sure if he had another brother, himself and Emily would be put out of the farm and he would have had to make a living doing God knows what. Nonetheless he had an ache in his heart for the loss of a father, and at how bitter his father was over his choice of a wife. Noel felt a heavy burden. He and Emily both decided not to attend either churches while this uproar was going on. They found it very hard. They were the talk of the parish.

Tonight was going to be a big night, a night to catch up with all the gossip and everything else that was going on in the parish. Noel and herself were going to enjoy every minute of it, and looked forward to meeting up with all the girls. Noel's mum offered to babysit and give them a much-needed break. Bertie didn't agree with her helping Noel out. He had said so on more than one occasion, seething with rage. Miriam didn't know how much longer she could take it. She seemed to spend more time crying in the bathroom over the whole damn mess. She missed Winifred and what might have been. But she loved Emily now, and her lovely grandchildren. Her home no longer felt like a home. There was no laughter in the house anymore.

With the excitement of the party, Emily wondered if she should buy a dress from Siobhan's shop? She wasn't sure what she had in her wardrobe. She could hardly fit one more garment into her already very full wardrobe. She hardly ever went out these days. But her friend Charlotte had plenty of nice dresses and maybe she would lend her one for the party as they were the same size. Emily had lost all the baby weight, with all the coming and going, which wasn't at all surprising.

Charlotte's cousin Lucinda worked in St Andrew's Hospital in Clontarf in Dublin. She decided to grace Charlotte with her presence for the weekend. Lucinda lived the highlife in Dublin and was a very outgoing girl. She was glad of the break from the city now and again, 'just to recharge the batteries'.

Someone to Rely On

Elizabeth and Paddy asked Anne, one of the local girls, to babysit for a couple of hours. Both families were good friends and lived nearby. Anne was a girl who could be trusted to mind the house and to babysit their precious Mikey. But Mikey wasn't at all pleased with the idea of some girl minding him. She wasn't just some girl. He knew her well. She was more like a big sister who treated him like her little brother. She spent a lot of time coming and going from his house with her mother and it wasn't the first time that she babysat for him. Sure, wasn't he big enough anyway to mind the house when his mammy and daddy were out for a couple of hours? After all he was eleven years old and not a child. His daddy decided to give him some jobs to do around the farm. Mickey felt very grown up and was delighted that his daddy trusted him.

'Sure, isn't he the big man,' said his father, going off to the party. 'He's a big man now who can be relied on.'

The party was in full swing in the back of the pub and everybody was in top form. As well as enjoying the party Rose and Johnny were on duty, and were delighted with the business coming their way and not to the Country Hotel. They knew their place wasn't as grand but by the time they had got it ready for the party, you couldn't tell the difference between their place and the hotel.

Rose and Johnny had six children, some of them young adults. They hoped the younger ones might follow Cormack and Rebecca, who were in college. They were snug enough but didn't have, as Rose would say, 'plenty of money or anything of the sort!' Rose always reminded her children to cut corners if necessary and not to pick up fair-weather friends who were leeches and looking for a free ride throughout life.

'Avoid the type who empty out everyone else's pockets and never their own,' John would say to his children, 'getting whatever was on offer. Remember not all people you will come across will be like you. Don't be mean with your money when with friends but know who their friends are and don't ever forget how hard you work for your few bob!'

Mary asked her daddy if the drawing for Meme was nice. Her father said that he had never ever seen anything like it. Mary had painted Madge and Bernard looking like they were having a nice time at the party, both with a glass of milk and some chocolate biscuits. Mary's father, Frank, sat down beside Madge and Bernard at the party. He had something important to ask Madge and wondered how to go about it and if he should ask them straight out. She might think he expected too much of her. He would give her whatever money that was needed of course, so he hoped what he had to ask Madge would come across alright.

Noel and Emily, Charlotte, Siobhan, Lucinda and Sarah were in great form at the party. They had all met up with Tom and Ellen, and Lorraine and Terence. Bronwyn came over for a quick chat and to see how everyone was getting on. She loved to hear a bit of news and what better occasion for a bit of gossip. Not that she was nosy or anything of the sort!

Lucinda, full of chat, said she always looked forward to coming down to the country for the odd weekend, but was sure she couldn't live here all the time. Village life was way too quiet for her.

'My thoughts exactly!' Sarah piped up.

'Why not come up to Dublin?' Lucinda suggested. 'There's plenty of work in the hospital where I work. What do you think?'

Sarah decided that it was time to make the move, and Bronwyn agreed that she has been restless and unhappy for a long time. She would miss the little featherhead as she was very fond of her. But she knew Sarah had to make her way into the big world and would never be content to settle down in the country, for now at least.

A Time for Change

So, the time was right for Sarah to move away from home and everybody she had grown up with. She was going to miss everyone. It wouldn't be like when she was away training to be a nurse. She had come home often and when she couldn't get home her mother and father would make the trip in their car, bringing her home-cooked food and her favourite rhubarb tart. This time it was going to be a different kind of journey as she made her way out in the big world on her own.

Bronwyn dropped in some holy medals and a prayer book, and a beautiful card wishing her all the luck in the world. Bronwyn promised her mother that she would be included in her prayer list every Sunday, for God and His Holy Mother's protection to keep her safe. She gave Sarah a big hug. Then Bronwyn was gone. She couldn't stay any longer as Sarah would see the tears streaming down her face. It was a side of her she would never let anyone see. Bronwyn felt she had to be the strong one in every situation.

Sarah knew it was time to cut the apron strings and, with mixed emotions, she rubbed the tears from her eyes. Bronwyn didn't hide her distress as well as she thought she had. Sarah knew she was going to miss her. She was like a second mammy to her.

She began to pack. She had decided not to take all her clothes. They might not be fashionable enough for Dublin. She would pop over to Siobhan and pick out a special party dress. Maybe she could buy one like those Audrey Hepburn wore in *Roman Holiday* or what Maureen O'Hara and the other Hollywood style queens wore at the première of their movies. Dublin would be the best place to buy new clothes, she thought, as she became more like her old self. It was going to be a time for adventure, a new chapter in her life. With all those butterflies in her tummy, she could barely finish her packing.

Characters in the Parish

'I know now why he is called Big John,' Madge said to her husband Bernard. 'It's because of all that fatty bacon and pounds of butter and whatever else he cooks on that frying pan of his. No wonder he can't get a woman to watch out for him!'

Madge had heard a young one asking her mammy in the shop the other day why John's big backside had moved around to his front. Bernard had laughed heartily and said,

'Hasn't he a huge belly and no acre at all!'

Not a day went by that her husband didn't make her laugh. They could both always see the funny side of a situation but were never unkind or harmed anyone.

'Maybe it's not too late for him to get a good woman,' Madge said to Bernard, 'though there aren't too many left around these parts, only Maggie and Peggy, that is if they were out of jail. But you wouldn't wish either of them on your worst enemies and definitely not on Big John.'

Fair Day in the Village

Rose and Johnny got their fair share of business after the market, with the farmers catching up on who had gotten the best prices for their animals. Some of their children would wait outside of the pub, gorging on Marietta biscuits and drinking bottles of orange to keep them content. They were happy too to play games like marbles and horseshoes. The market was a social outing for many parishioners, though it left an awful mess in the village and a stink from the animals. It usually took a few days to get the place back in order. All the businesses in Kilton did well on fair day.

CHAPTER TWENTY-SEVEN

The Request

Madge was in the kitchen having a cup of tea when the doorbell rang. Bernard answered the door to find Frank, Mary's father, standing outside. Frank asked if Madge was in and if he could have a word with her.

'Sure Frank, you know at this stage you are one of us,' said Bernard and led him into the warm kitchen.

Madge wondered if everything was alright. Frank just came out with it then.

'Madge,' he said, 'I was wondering if you would help Mary pick out a dress for her communion?'

Madge nearly choked on the biscuit she was eating as she couldn't believe her ears.

'I beg your pardon could you repeat that?'

Frank got very embarrassed and apologised for putting her in an awkward situation.

'Oh, don't apologise, Frank! After all the years longing to have children of my own, I'd thought that part of life had passed me by. It would be an honour to help in dressing Mary for this special occasion.'

She loved this little girl and Mary loved her Meme. Madge felt so maternal each time Mary called her that. The child loved making cakes with Madge in her big spacious kitchen, and feeding Goldie, Bernard's cocker spaniel, with sweet mashed dough.

Madge promised Mary a treat in the tea shop after they had bought the most beautiful dress they had ever seen along with everything to match. Mary bopped all over the place with excitement.

'Meme, how many more weeks before I can wear my lovely dress?'

Rose met up with Madge and Mary in the dress shop. Rose wanted to buy Mary her bag as she also wanted her to have an extra special day. As Rose had many children of her own, she thought she could have a little input into Mary's special occasion, and could also point Madge in the right direction as she didn't have children of her own. The child was loved and wanted by Madge, Bernard and Rose, and of course her doting father, Frank. Rose, with a twinkle in her eye, would call Mary her 'outside daughter' and had no problem in helping Madge and Frank out if she was needed.

After a lovely day of shopping and with everything bought, Frank wanted to give Madge the money for it all. Madge told him that it was to be her treat, and of course Rose had insisted on buying Mary her bag.

Madge and Bernard were involved in everything to do with Mary's communion day. Mary Jenkins, one of the local girls, was more than happy to work for Bernard and Madge for four or five hours on this special day. The nuns put on a big breakfast in the convent every year for the children of the parish, and afterwards they were brought around the convent grounds where they kept goldfish in a very large pond. There was great excitement as they walked around the lovely gardens with the scent of all the beautiful flowers. The stalls were set up outside the church gates, with everything from butterscotch and pineapple bars, Peggy's legs and bullseyes. There were even ice cream and ice lollipops there, kept cold in a big ice box. The children looked at the stalls in amazement. Mary wished this day could last forever and didn't want it to end.

She knew her mammy was up in heaven and looking down on her. Her daddy and the nuns would tell her that she was special to have a mammy in heaven but Mary wished with all her heart that her mammy would come down from heaven just for one day if God would let her.

Suddenly Mary was brought back to reality when she heard Madge calling her name. She was so glad that Meme was her mammy now, she loved her so much. Frank was delighted they got on so well and never minded her staying over with Madge on the odd night. Frank himself was an only child. Both his parents and his wife Gertrude were dead. He was rearing his young daughter on his own.

Madge and Bernard were very glad to make Frank and Mary part of their family. Over time everything just slotted into place, as Bernard and himself became not just friends, but like father and son.

A Good Deed for the Undeserving

Ross was on his way over to Paddy and Rose's pub after school, when he heard someone call his name. He wondered who the heavens it could be as he turned around to look. Charlotte was waving frantically at him. He had left his briefcase behind in the corridor of the school, and it was a Friday evening so he wouldn't be able to get it until Monday as the school would be locked up.

Ross had been distracted this past while, with his only hope of making a good match and of getting a good wife gone for now. He kept asking himself how he could have been so stupid and why had he waited so long. Any one of the three women would have done; well, maybe Ellen would have been the last on his list. She was the only woman that he loved, but he simply couldn't let sentiment spoil his future. He could have got together with Sarah, but that wasn't going to happen now as she had left to work in Dublin, so that was the end of that.

Charlotte, a fiery redhead with lots of freckles, was a colleague of Ross's. She stood up to Ross in school and wouldn't let him away with anything. He was always right, never wrong. Charlotte, on the other hand would wait to be proven right. She was very patient, and often she was usually on the right track.

Ross thanked her for bringing his briefcase to him. It contained all the pupils' homework for correction. The copybooks had to be ready for Monday morning as the examiner would be in the school early. He would have been seen as lazy and incompetent by the principal if the work wasn't done.

Ross offered to bring Charlotte into Rose's pub for a sherry or shandy to thank her. They hardly ever agreed on anything, but in truth she didn't have a mean bone in her body. She was the daughter of a legal secretary who worked for a local solicitor, and her father was the headmaster of the primary school over in Ballycash. Ross liked her fiery temper and got on well with her most of the time. He often thought she would have made a great suffragette back in the day and was cut out for politics. She had a lot of passion, knew what was right and always fought for the underdog. Ross found himself drawn to her more and more but he felt the time wasn't right. She would have to show some sort of interest in him first, but he felt that was unlikely.

CHAPTER TWENTY-EIGHT

A Doctor in the House

'For goodness sake, Cormac, you need to concentrate on what you are doing!' said Johnny, scolding his son after he had dropped a large bottle of whiskey on the cement floor.

Cormac was a tall redhead and had deliberated long and hard about what he wanted to do with his future. When he remembered his school days, he thought of when he was brought for whatever injection he needed, and how he loved the smell of the dispensary and looking at all the medicine bottles. He would ask Doctor Cantwell questions about everything from the needles to the tablets. Of course Sadie, who was the stern-looking nurse in charge of the dispensary, would have none of it. It hadn't mattered whether you were nervous or not, she would just grab you and stick the needle in your arm. Cormac knew it was a job that had to be done, so there was no use in whining. But his friend Marty would always have a nervous giggling fit, then turn green and faint at the nurse's feet, much to Sadie's annoyance.

Johnny and Rose were frugal. Each of the boys, and Rebecca, their only girl, were savers and not a bit afraid of doing some work, stacking bottles and cleaning the pub when the doors were closed. Johnny made sure that they didn't shy away from work. They would need survival skills out in the big world, Johnny would tell Rose. For birthdays and other occasions each child used different skills for making up presents. Between them they could make up something nice that didn't cost a lot, not that they were mean. Rose had always said that type of present came from the heart.

A Warm Sunny Day

Madge said it had been a lovely day and everything had gone so well.

'What I can say about Mother Veronica and Mother Rita,' she told Bronwyn and Rose over a pot of tea, 'they really made a fuss of the little ones and looked after them like old mother hens.'

Madge had enjoyed herself every bit as much as Mary, if not more. She continued to tell her friends how the nuns had dressed Kitty Gaynor's daughter, Biddy, from her underwear, shoes, dress and veil to even her bag, with Mother Mary putting a shilling and a lace handkerchief in it.

The women felt guilty then for not helping the family.

'Sugar!' Rose said. 'Why didn't we think of it? Well, we won't forget it again in future, girls.'

They felt sorry for Kitty Gaynor after the tragedy in the family but everybody knew that late husband of hers was no good and hoped that she was glad to be rid of him. The worst part of it all was TJ had looked up to his father, who had led him down the same road to jail. But now maybe all wouldn't be lost and there would be justice at last for Kitty and her children.

CHAPTER TWENTY-NINE

Great Excitement

Tom and Ellen were delighted to tell their friends their exciting news. They laughed about their sleepless nights, and the ups and downs, the big changes a baby was going to bring in their lives.

'It isn't going to be all about us anymore,' Ellen and Tom said to their parents. 'It will be a time of great joy in the family.'

Ellen's mother-in-law brought over a pram, which was as good as new, and a cot and playpen that had belonged to Tom and his older sister, Theresa. Tom's mother said there was nothing like a freshly painted room and that it gave you a sense of spring. She was so delighted she was going to be a grandmother at last. If she was waiting for her daughter Theresa she would be waiting for ever. Theresa was far too busy with her career. She had a top position in a busy hospital, so for now it would have to be Tom she would rely on for grandchildren.

Tom's mother was counting down the days and was always on the lookout for anything new in the market for her first grandchild. She would call in to Ellen with a load of books, showing her all kinds of new gadgets, and usually had a little something in her bag for when baby arrived. She always had a bar of chocolate for her daughter-in-law; she was very happy to have her in the family, as they got on so well.

Ellen wanted the colour of the nursery to be a soft primrose, trimmed off with a blue and pink flower. Tom agreed that was a good idea and that whether they had a boy or girl, they couldn't go wrong.

'Look what happened to Emily with her blue cake,' he laughed. 'No, we won't be making the same mistake!'

Ellen asked Emily what she should buy for the hospital.

'Let's see now,' said her friend, 'you will need at least six long cotton dresses and the same number of blankets.'

Ellen's mother was knitting up a storm, and yellow, blue, white and pink were the order of the day. She was very good at embroidery and made a beautiful eiderdown for her grandchild's pram. Emily packed the case for Ellen, and packed six of everything. She also included baby powder, Vaseline, cotton wool and whatever Ellen herself needed. The case was left in the hall, ready to go.

The Loneliest Time

At half past eleven on the Thursday morning, Ellen became very restless, knowing that although she had ten weeks left to go, there was no mistaking very sharp pains. Suddenly, her underclothes were soaking wet, though she didn't want to use the lavatory. She rang Emily in a major panic. Her friend dropped everything, and asked her mother Erin to take over until she got back, half filling her in on the details on the way out.

Ellen was telling her what had happened when all of a sudden she fell to the ground, bleeding and unable to stand with the pain. Emily rang Bronwyn and told her to come quick. Bronwyn knew it was far too early for the baby to come. She rushed out of the dispensary, telling everyone to come back at nine in the morning.

Bronwyn was very worried but she never panicked. It was important not to let Ellen see the worry on her face and to keep calm. Tom managed to get Ellen into bed with the help of Emily and Bronwyn. Then Tom's father, Dr John Mc Govern, arrived. Suddenly Ellen wanted to push. Bronwyn tried to hold her back but no matter what the doctor and Bronwyn did or said, they couldn't stop the little baby from being born. Bronwyn, though worried that it was too early, hoped everything would be all right.

The baby didn't cry. Both nurse and doctor did everything possible for the little mite, a girl. Emily felt an overwhelming feeling of helplessness, but tried to stay strong for Ellen, as she held onto her and Tom, tears streaming down their faces. Bronwyn and the child's grandfather were still trying to get the baby to breathe, but Dr John knew the baby had a lot of problems and that it was impossible to save his tiny grandchild.

Emily waited for Ellen's parents and her mother-in-law to arrive before she made her way home to Noel and her beautiful girls. Both Noel and

Emily shed heavy tears for their friends, and what might have been. It was just not meant to be this time.

Ellen went into a deep depression. She couldn't sleep at night thinking of her little darling daughter lying in a closed box instead of her cot, lying there in a cold grave when she should be snug and warm at home with her mother and father. Ellen felt she should go to the graveyard and bring her baby home. She thought, what kind of mother would leave her child lying in the cold ground with no mammy and daddy to love her? She knew what she was thinking just wasn't normal, yet as a mother it was natural to feel this way.

Tom was woken in the middle of the night to the noise of drawers being opened and closed. As he rubbed the sleep from his eyes, he could just about see Ellen pulling out jumpers and trying to dress herself at the same time. She kept saying, 'I have to bring her home, Tom! We can't leave her there!'

Tom started to cry, broken-hearted with the loss of his daughter. He tried to calm Ellen down, but he could hardly manage to calm himself. He went downstairs to get a sedative and a glass of water for his poor grieving Ellen.

Emily and Charlotte spent a lot of time with Ellen. Madge would bring over all the gossip that was happening in the parish, funny stories and mad stories, trying to get a smile out her, and Bronwyn also made regular house calls. Eventually Ellen started going back out to the shops again and trying to get back to some kind of normality. She has been in a dark fog for a long time, but now she was glad to see the light once again. She couldn't stop apologising to Tom, wondering how he put up with her. What she didn't realise was that Tom loved her no matter what and she would rest in his arms always.

Her mum heard Ellen talking to herself in the bedroom while she was putting the baby clothes away.

'Where is the yellow cardigan? I am also missing a cotton dress and booties.'

As soon as the words were out of her mouth she knew the baby was buried in them. 'At least she had her granny's lovingly-knitted clothes on her.' The tears rolled down her face as she sobbed, asking her mother if she was going mad. Ellen knew her thoughts weren't normal. Her mother went in to her bedroom to comfort her grieving daughter, holding her as they both cried for the loss of their little baby girl.

Noel met up with Tom from time to time for the odd pint of Guinness, to give him some support. He knew he wasn't managing very well. Make no mistake, Tom could hide his feelings quite well. But Noel knew him better than anyone else. They were close friends and had gone to school together. As young lads, they had lived in each other's houses, swapping comics. They pair of them were always up to something, playing pranks on each other. Noel tried to spend some time with him, until he could cope. Tom thought how everyone needed a friend like Noel. Friendship made life more bearable when you found yourself in unfortunate circumstances of one kind or another.

Madge had to make a call to the chemist to pick up a prescription for Bernard. She was very pleased to see Tom behind the counter. She asked how Ellen was doing today. Madge and the rest of the friends were back and forward to Ellen's house a lot. Tom said she was getting there, thanks to all of them, and wondered what they would have done without their friends.

'We are all on the mend, including both sets of our parents. The sun is beginning to shine once again, Madge,' he sighed. 'We are so grateful for everyone's kindness at such an awful time. Thanks again, Madge, for being there for us.'

'Why wouldn't I, Tom?' said a tearful Madge. 'Ellen has been such a part of my life from a young girl. Bernard and I love her very much.'

CHAPTER THIRTY

The Edge of Teen Years

Mary was twelve years old and looking forward to secondary school. But Meme had to remind her that she hadn't quite left primary school just yet. After all, there was the little matter of her confirmation, she joked. Mary was delighted with the gorgeous clothes that Meme had picked out for her to wear, though there were still the shoes to buy. She said, with a big smile,

'What about the black patent shoes in Burke's window?' She had seen them the previous morning on the way to school, and hadn't been able to stop thinking about them. If only she could buy them before someone else did. She knew she had to try them on.

Madge brought Mary down to the shop the next day. There was a half-day from school for the confirmation children. Mary looked in the window but there was no sign of the shoes. Meme told her not to worry, and that she was sure the shoes would be inside. She could see the disappointment in the child's face.

Mr Burke greeted Madge and the young girl at the door, then asked them to take a seat and he would bring down whatever shoes he had in her size that would be suitable for such an occasion. They tried on at least ten pairs of shoes to no avail. By now they were tired, and a cup of tea was needed in the worst way.

They decided to give up and go down to the tea shop. Madge felt it was time for a sticky bun and a pink lemonade to help Mary get over the disappointment of not getting the shoes. It was time then to go home.

Bernard had a chicken cooking in the oven and hoped Frank would be home in time for dinner. He wanted to talk to him about the match that was to take place in Dublin between Tipperary and Cork. That would be a match worth seeing, if Madge would let him off for the Sunday. Bernard wondered how was he going to get around her.

Madge heard a knock on the door. When she answered, she found Mr

Burke on the doorstep. Madge was delighted to see him. He had brought over another three boxes of shoes for the young child to try on. Mary scrambled off the sofa, pulling off her shoes at the same time. He opened the top off the first box, to reveal plain black shoes, that looked like boy's shoes, Mary thought. Madge peeped into the other boxes. She pushed a blue one towards Mary, lifting off the lid slowly. Mary couldn't be calmed down for at least an hour after she saw the black patent shoes. Mrs Burke had put them away for another child, but they had been too small for her.

Mary tried on her new uniform for secondary school, a navy gym slip, white blouse and red tie. That little bit of red set the uniform off nicely.

'Bernard!' called Madge. 'Come in here for a minute. Just take a quick look at this princess, with her lovely dark hair and those green eyes. Well, do you like her uniform?' Madge looked over at Mary, who had lost her puppy fat and become a lovely tall girl, who was not short in the looks department. She was like her own daughter and she treated her likewise, though putting down boundaries when necessary. Frank was forever grateful to Madge and Bernard for their love and kindness,

A Shocking Time in the Parish

Bernard answered the phone. Johnny asked him to come over to talk about some urgent business with Michael, the local guard. Bernard rushed towards the door while Madge called after him.

'You can't go and leave sacks of spuds and vegetables in the middle of the shop floor, Bernard! We have to have it sorted before morning.'

She spoke in a low voice, not making too much noise, as Mary was asleep upstairs. Bernard shouted back, 'I won't be long, Madge. The lads need to talk to me. It sounds urgent!'

Madge had asked Frank about buying a chip cutter from the hardware store next time he was in Dublin. She couldn't get one in the village hardware store, as they didn't have a big supply of new merchandise. She thought the chip cutter was a great thing for making chips. They were all the rage according to Rose. All she'd have to do is to peel the potatoes and the cutter would do the rest. Rose said she wouldn't be without it, and all the children just loved their spuds cooked that way.

Frank bought the chip cutter for Madge and had left it in his car. He had one last call to make to the jeweller's for a confirmation present for his daughter. It was a gold chain with her name engraved on it, and her mother's name and his engraved on the back. The shop assistant was very helpful, placing it in a special red box.

This was a special time for his young daughter, his one and only child who held his heart. He also bought some cufflinks for Bernard and a gold chain and cross for Madge to thank them for all their kindness. He felt he could never thank them enough. They had always treated him like the son they never had. Bernard looked out for him, and offered advice if it was needed without pushing his opinion too much on Frank.

Before Frank set off home, he thought he would have his tea back at the hotel where he usually stayed whenever he was up in Dublin. Frank was feeling very pleased with himself and wondering what his late wife would have thought of their lovely daughter. He had never loved another woman. It had always been Gertrude.

Frank didn't see the bus coming towards him, as he was so deep in thought. The drivers kept beeping their horns, but he didn't hear them. Next thing he was on the ground, with people all round him, asking if he could hear them and if he was alright. The ambulance arrived and he was lifted onto a stretcher. The doctor couldn't feel a pulse. The ambulance sped through the city, winding its way to the nearest hospital. The nurses and doctors did all they could but it didn't make any difference. They had lost the young man. The ambulance men searched his pockets for clues as to who he was and where he was from. They found the gold chains and cufflinks inside his breast pocket, along with his wallet and a receipt with the name of the hotel where he was staying. The guards went to the hotel to check his luggage. They found his car with his briefcase inside it.

Michael, Johnny and Bernard arrived back to the shop. Rose followed behind just as they were about to sit down. Madge wondered what was going on. Had something happened in the parish? Rose made her way in to the kitchen to make a pot of tea and strong black coffee. Being one of Madge's closest friends, she knew her way around, so it wouldn't be at all unusual.

Michael had already told Johnny what had happened. Bernard was ashen-faced and kept saying, 'I don't believe it. Are they sure?'

Madge sat in silence for a few minutes and couldn't move with the shock. Then she heard an unmerciful cry and wondered where it was coming from, when all sudden she realised it was from her. Rose jumped out of the chair, crying, and ran over to her friend trying to comfort her.

Rose went to the convent the next morning to see Mary's teacher and explain what had happened. The conformation was only a week away, and everything was put on hold for Mary. She wouldn't be at any rehearsals and would be out of school for a while.

Madge went upstairs to get Mary, who jumped up out of bed, always in good form. Madge would have her breakfast ready when she got up and Bernard would pack a lunch for her on the days that she stayed over, and always put in a little surprise for her without telling Meme. But of course, she knew it was a game, and always appreciated their love and kindness. This time Madge and Bernard brought her in to the sitting room. Madge, Rose and Bronwyn sat down with Mary. Madge told Mary that her daddy had had an accident in Dublin, and was knocked down crossing the road. The guards had brought him to hospital but he died, though they had done everything they could to save him. The medical team were always upset at such tragedy, which left them powerless at such a loss.

Mary started to cry and didn't say anything for a while. Meme just cuddled her, while Rose made her a mug of hot chocolate. Bernard sat beside her, holding her hand. He and Madge started to cry with her, for the loss of a good father and friend.

Madge and Bernard organised some help in the shop for at least a week and ordered whatever was needed from their suppliers to keep the shop going. Father Rory helped the Byrnes to organise the funeral. It was hard to understand how such a thing could happen. He had been so young and was leaving behind his only child, now an orphan.

On arriving back to Kilton the undertaker asked Madge and Bernard if Mary would want to see her father one last time. They agreed not, as they felt she couldn't possibly take in such a sight and it was important for the child to remember him smiling and being full of fun. This was best for her.

The family, meaning Madge, Bernard, Mary, Noel, Tom, and Frank's many friends, arrived at the graveside. The four girls, Emily, Siobhan, Ellen and Charlotte stood close to Madge and Bernard, close enough to put their arms on their shoulders to try and lessen their pain, but they knew that was impossible. Mary was still not saying very much but crying a lot. She looked up at Madge and grabbed her as though never to let her go.

'Oh, Mammy! What are we going to do without Daddy?'

Madge started to cry, for indeed she was her mammy now! It was the first time she had ever been called by that name. Bernard was broken-hearted at the loss of Frank. How would he cope without him? He had loved him and treated him like a son and he knew Frank had felt the same way about him.

The following days went by in a haze. Mary wasn't speaking at all. Her friend, Rebecca, spent whatever time she could with her young friend. Rebecca was making her confirmation in a couple of days and was feeling very bad about that. How was she going to go to the chapel without Mary? Rebecca told her that in one way she was lucky to have Madge for her mammy and this was her house now. But Mary thought only about the pain in her chest. It felt like she couldn't breathe. She was too young to realise that she was suffering from a broken heart. Suddenly, she started to cry very loudly, saying, 'Oh, my Daddy, my Daddy! Don't leave me!' Then she wept softly into her pillow. Rebecca went downstairs to Madge and Bernard, and told them about her best friend, with tears running down her cheeks. She wondered if she could put her confirmation off and make it with Mary in a couple of months' time, as Fr Rory had said Mary could do.

'You are a good friend Rebecca,' said Bernard. 'You are so young to understand all the pain she is suffering. Sit down, love, and I'll get you a mug of chocolate and a slice of chocolate cake before I walk you home.'

But he didn't have to, as Rebecca's mother arrived, knowing that the two friends were going through a traumatic time. She would do whatever she could do for the young girls. Rebecca only lived down the road.

All four turned around to see Mary standing in the doorway. Madge walked towards her young daughter and wrapped her arms around her. Bernard put his arm on her shoulder and told her to sit down and have some hot chocolate. She hadn't let a bite of food past her mouth in nearly a week. Only time would bring her around, said Rebecca's mother with a quiver in her voice.

Mother Veronica knocked on Madge and Bernard's door.

'We were wondering,' she said, 'that is, Father Rory and the rest of us, if Mary might like to make her confirmation with her friend Rebecca and the rest of her school friends. We understand that she might like to wait for a few months and make it on her own. Fr Rory said we can also arrange it that way.'

Rebecca jumped up from the table. It was only two days away. Mary stood up and walked over to Mother Veronica while holding Madge's hand. She told Mother Veronica that she would like to make her confirmation with her friend, adding, 'If that's is alright with you, Mammy?'

Bernard and Madge hugged their young charge.

'We have everything ready,' said Madge. 'The only thing left to do is to arrange extra help for the shop, then we can take the whole day off! Maybe we might go to that fancy café in Wicklow town where all the teenagers go for malt milkshakes. What do you think about that?'

Rebecca and her mammy said that they would all go to Wicklow as a nice treat and very different from celebrating the confirmation at home. Rebecca held Mary's hand and gave her a big hug.

She said, 'I will see you in the morning! Friends forever, Mary, you and me, friends forever.'

Michael called to the door of Bernard and Madge's shop with a parcel. It was Frank's belongings, along with his briefcase and whatever else they had taken from his car, before it was taken in to the garage for Bernard, the child's guardian, to collect.

How Do You Sum Up a Life?

Charlotte, Rose and Emily began the hard task of clearing out Frank's house. They had to decide what to save for Mary and what should go to the charity shop. Charlotte collected loads of boxes for clothes, pots, pans and all the things that make up a home. Emily called Rose into the bedroom to help sort out Frank's clothes. He had three navy suits, two black pairs of slacks and one pair of blue jeans, all in very good condition, and quite a few shirts and sweaters. The girls began to get upset. They still couldn't grasp the reality of the tragedy and the ending of a young life.

Charlotte continued to pack the clothes neatly into boxes as if Frank was going to wear them again. She just couldn't throw them into an old bag. They must be very careful with these special clothes and she hoped the right people would get them, and they wouldn't end up wasted on someone who wouldn't appreciate them.

'What will we do with all his hurling clothes, girls?' she asked the others. She asked Rose then if she knew anyone that would like them.

'I think Bernard would like to keep them in a separate box with his name on it,' Rose answered.

The girls opened the presses to find cards that Frank had given to his wife and she to him on special occasions. Emily felt like she was snooping in their private lives, plans for their future and their hopes and dreams. Reading the cards, some soppy, some funny, the girls could see how much they loved each other. The tears streamed down Emily's face as she thought about what might have been. It all got too much for the women. It was time to take a break.

The women made their way up to Madge for a strong pot of tea. They brought along the cards and letters, and anything else that might be important for young Mary later. Madge would put them up on top of her wardrobe to keep them safe, along with Frank's hurl and sports clothes for Bernard.

Oliver helped with bringing some of the boxes over to the charity shop, cutting the grass and whatever else he could do for the women. He had liked poor auld Frank, as had everybody in the village and the wider parishes. He had sold insurance to the local people, and a nicer man you just wouldn't meet. Oliver had gotten on with him, sport being their main topic of conversation whenever they had met up.

A Day to Endure

The confirmation day arrived. Mary wore her beautiful yellow dress with a cream cardigan and the black patent shoes. She looked very pale, with her long dark hair framing her little face and making her deep green eyes stand out.

'You look lovely, Mary,' Madge told her, 'and have no doubt that your mammy and daddy are looking down from heaven right now.'

Everything went well. You couldn't call it a great day, not even a good day. It was a day that had to be got through. Rebecca did all that she could do for her best friend. Finally, Madge, Bernard and Mary arrived home. Madge said she would be back in a minute while Bernard put on the kettle. Mary looked up at her mammy, who was holding a little red box, which contained the gold chain Frank had bought for her confirmation.

Mary looked at the back and front of the heart-shaped locket, and at her parent's names engraved on it. Tears rolled down her pale little face. It was important that she received this special gift on her confirmation day. But it would have been too upsetting to give it to her this morning.

'Mary, you will always know where you came from,' said Madge, 'and who your parents were.'

Madge settled her down for the night giving her the biggest hug ever, and, with a heavy heart, returned to the sitting room for a cup of tea. Bernard brought in the parcel that Sergeant Michael had given to them. Madge cried as they opened it. In the parcel was the chip cutter Frank had bought for her in Dublin, along with the other lovely gifts for them, as well as the rest of his personal belongings. It was time for Bernard to sort out Frank's affairs and to get in touch with his place of work to make sure all his customers had been notified of his death so they could rearrange their insurance with the company.

CHAPTER THIRTY-ONE

New Expectations

Ellen and Tom went to St Anne's hospital in Dublin, two weeks before the baby was due. Ellen had felt a few twinges and knew something was happening. She was afraid to wait at home. They arrived, bag packed, at the hospital in just over an hour, with their parents not far behind them.

The doctor and nurses were waiting for them the hallway. They were aware of Ellen's history so weren't going to take any chances. After examining Ellen, it was confirmed that she was in labour. Tom started to panic. He fainted where his parents were standing. His father, being a doctor, knew it was nerves after the loss of their baby daughter, a much-wanted child. When he came around, the nurses and his father helped him onto a chair and gave him a mug of sweet tea.

After waiting for a couple of hours the doctor finally came out to the hall and called Tom. Tom could hardly stand up. His father helped him up. The doctor told Tom that there was no need to worry.

'You have a fine little boy, with all his toes and fingers, and a good pair of lungs,' continued the doctor. 'Everything went well both for your wife and the child!'

The parents of Ellen and Tom couldn't contain their excitement. After making sure everything was alright, they set off to the nearby hotel and ordered a bottle of vintage champagne.

The first call Tom made was to Noel and Emily. He asked Noel to pass on the good news to all their friends. It was the best news ever. Nobody could wait to see the young couple. It was a time of great joy in the village.

Ellen arrived home from the hospital with her new baby. She couldn't understand why she wasn't brimming over with joy like Tom and their parents. One minute she was overjoyed, the next she was overcome by guilt for feeling so happy after letting her baby daughter die. She over-did it when expecting her daughter, hanging up those heavy curtains on her own. Why couldn't she have waited for Emily, who promised to give her a hand? Ellen had wanted her home to look well for visitors when she arrived home with her baby. She hadn't been able to relax, everything had had to be neat and tidy, right down to her suitcase, checking and rechecking she had packed everything. At one stage, she thought she should have packed a toothbrush for baby! She had thought she must have been losing the plot. But she and Tom had a good laugh at the idea of a new baby with a toothbrush. At the same time, he had told his wife to put her feet up and take it easy.

Ellen stood in the middle of her kitchen holding an empty saucepan, her baby son crying out to be fed. But she couldn't move, overwhelmed by the loss of her daughter. She flung the saucepan across the room and it landed at the door, barely missing Tom. He was shocked at Ellen. This behaviour wasn't at all like her and he knew something was wrong.

'You should be happy, Ellen! Look over at our lovely son,' he cried.

She dropped to her knees, buried her head in her hands and began to sob uncontrollably. The empty hole in her heart was wide open and she wondered how she was ever going to fix it.

What Tom hadn't realized is that you can't replace one baby for another. At that very moment, Tom's mother walked into the room to see Ellen in that dreadful state. She rushed over to help her daughter-in-law up and led her gently to a chair. Tom could hardly move at witnessing such a scene, so upset was he.

'Put the kettle on, Tom,' said his mother, 'and make a strong pot of tea.' His mother couldn't comfort Ellen. She left her with Tom for a few min-utes and went downstairs to phone Ellen's own mother.

Ellen's parents arrived to see what they could do for their fragile daughter. When everything had calmed down, with Ellen settled in bed after taking a couple of sedatives, both mothers spoke to Tom. They said that between them they would take care of Ellen and the baby.

Ellen was going through a nervous breakdown and was moved to hospital to convalesce. Tom was told that it would take some time. Emily, Charlotte, Siobhan, even Sarah when she came home for the weekend, took turns in helping their friend back to health.

A Time to Heal

Joseph, Bronwyn's old friend, came home for a holiday. It was really an excuse to see Bronwyn. He had been ill for quite a while, but now was back in form once again. He knew he had to deal with some unfinished business with his dear old friend Bronwyn. He had a lot of time to think in hospital. It was now time to make amends. He knew that Bronwyn loved him, but he also knew that he could never return her love. He wasn't attracted to her in that way or to any other woman, for that matter. Joseph had felt a strong pull towards his own sex since his days at boarding school. He thought those feelings wouldn't last, but he still felt the same after graduating from college. No girl could turn his head. He settled down in a good job in his own country for a few years. London was where he spent all his holidays. Now the time had come to make a permanent move out of Ireland, to live the life he wanted to live. He had met his lover many years ago, on one of his many trips.

Joseph and his partner were to move to France and to settle down in Paris. Both loved the city life and felt very comfortable in the world of actors, writers and designers.

Joseph's love for his partner was one he wasn't allowed to speak about. They could never have a life in the land of his birth. Joseph and his partner were very happy. He could never imagine having settled down with any women or being a parent. The time had come to tell Bronwyn about his sexuality. This holiday, he explained to his partner, was one he must make on his own.

Time Out for a Tired Soul

Bronwyn had just come back from doing her rounds. She gazed up at the clock as it chimed five times. She was delighted with the little extra time.

It was good to get home early now and again. She filled the bath up with lavender bubble bath, and breathed in the scent of fresh cotton towels. At the same time, she spoke out loud, wondering if she would have a salad with some fresh ham for tea? She wanted something quick and easy.

After the bath, she wrapped herself in a yellow fluffy bath towel. She thought that this was the nearest thing to a big hug and how she had forgotten what a real hug felt like. She put talcum powder in her hand and rubbed it in well all over her body. Bronwyn started talking to herself again, saying, it was time to get dressed now and stop pampering herself. Enough was enough.

After tea, she called over to Madge to catch up on all the gossip over a glass of sherry. Bernard put his head around the door, saying, 'Well now, ladies, sorry to disturb you both, but Bronwyn —'

The minute she heard her name being called, she let out a sigh.

'Don't worry, Bronwyn, it's not work. You have a gentleman caller.'

He opened the door and Bronwyn nearly fainted at the sight of her old friend Joseph. They embraced each other and were delighted to meet again after such a long time.

'You two must have some catching up to do,' said Madge.

Time to Make Amends

'The night is still young!' said Madge as she pushed her friend towards the door. 'I will catch up with you later!' she shouted after Bronwyn.

Joseph asked his old friend if they could go back to her place. He had so much to tell her. She listened attentively to Joseph as he told his story. When he had finished, Bronwyn started to cry, not for herself, but for all the pain he had been through and how he hadn't felt able to talk to her about it. No secret ever got out once it had been told to Bronwyn.

She was glad that he had finally opened up to her and at the knowledge that she hadn't been rejected. She understood that they had been the best of friends and their friendship could never have been anything more than that.

The People That Make a Difference in the Parish

Miss Susanne Foreman lived across the road from Mythen's public house. She was the daughter of the late Rev John Foreman. Everyone in the parish had liked him. He was a kind man to all the local people, no matter what their beliefs. They were all God's people. He spent his spare time, not that he had that much of that, fishing, and whatever he caught he would distribute amongst people in need. He never kept any fish for himself. Fishing was one of his favourite hobbies and he always complained that his free time went far too fast.

The local children would hang out of him when he came up from the river with his catch. He always had a few coppers which he would give to the children. If he didn't have money on him, he always had a bag of hard sweets in his pocket, so the children were looked after one way or another. He was almost like a father figure to the children of the parish who didn't have much of a father figure in their home life. Most of the local people were very sad when he died. Both Bernard and Madge agreed he had been a good man, would be a big loss to the parish.

The only ones that ever caused trouble were the two biddies, Peggy and Maggie. They caused big problems in the parish, always making remarks and sending up any Protestant from the area, calling them prodders. The Protestant community paid no heed to them or any other trouble-maker. Everyone knew they were always up to something, and nobody took a blind bit of notice. But at the same time, the people of minority faiths always watched their backs and never trusted the pot stirrers. But for now the locals didn't have to worry, as both women had ended up in prison for stealing from the parish and Siobhan's shop. People hoped they would come out of prison better people and have learned a big lesson.

Susanne was very like her father and popular with locals. Everybody liked her. At half past three every day she would go shopping, bringing Montgomery, her fluffy poodle, along for the walk. It was awfully long name for such a little dog, the locals would say, much to Susanne's amusement. Each day she would walk past the school gate and standing there would be her two little friends Emilia and Alana. They always called her by the name

Miss Susanne. It seemed so normal to the young girls to call her that. Most people called her Miss Susanne and it had stuck.

All three marched into Madge's shop with the dog. It always created pandemonium with the local children in buying sweets. The customers would hardly able to get in to do their shopping with all the fuss going on. Bernard couldn't handle more than four or five people in the shop at any one time. He usually got into a panic and his wife Madge would try to calm him down, saying, 'Miss Susanne is a valued customer. Now you have me calling her Miss Susanne! For goodness sake, Bernard! Don't you go and upset her now, do you hear me? Are you listening? Let one of the girls mind the damned thing outside the shop where he should be kept and let Miss Susanne or whatever the hell her name is get on with her shopping!'

'Honestly, Madge, we won't make a penny if this commotion carries on. That's the end of it, Madge!'

It was more like he was trying to convince himself as he said it.

Shortly afterwards he put up a large notice in the shop window. It banned all animals from the shop, big or small.

CHAPTER THIRTY-TWO

A Time to Reflect

Sarah arrived home for the weekend. She couldn't believe that she was looking forward to coming down the country. She had spent so much time trying to get out of the parish and away from the awful stink of silage! Sure, you couldn't go to the shops on market day with the smell all around you. She believed a long time ago that she was not cut out for country life. She had been home many times since she left for Dublin, and always looked forward to catching up on all the news.

Usually Madge's was her first stop, then Bronwyn, followed by her family. But this time it was different. She wanted to see Emily and her friends first. She had something on her mind. Madge knew Sarah too well and could tell that she had news.

'Well, what's happened?' Madge asked. 'Don't deny it!'

'Ah, Madge, I should have known you'd see through me!'

Sarah pulled off her glove to show off the cutest diamond ring Madge had ever seen.

'Who is he?! A doctor? For crying out loud, tell me, Sarah!'

'All will be revealed in time, Madge,' said Sarah, planting a kiss on Madge's cheek. Then she was gone before Madge had a chance to take it all in. Sarah went to show her ring to Emily, Charlotte, Siobhan and Ellen. They were so excited for Sarah! They guessed it had to be a Dublin man.

The girls made their way down to Madge's shop on Saturday evening. Madge could barely contain herself.

'Bernard, come here now for God's sake and hold the fort!' she shouted. 'I have very important business to discuss with the girls.'

They waited impatiently for Sarah to tell them all about her fiancé. Sarah had kept them in suspense long enough.

'You'll all have to wait another couple of weeks till I bring him down to meet you,' Sarah told them.

They were all deflated. It was time for tea and cake.

Sarah did indeed bring her beau down to the village. She knew she couldn't pass Madge's shop, as it was her usual first stop.

'Madge,' said Sarah, 'Pepa De Luca, my fiancé.'

Madge shook his hand, and at the same time noticed his smoke-stained fingers, oversized red linen jacket, primrose baggy pants, down to his well-worn brown shoes. Madge tried not to make it obvious she was inspecting him and giving him the once-over. He was a handsome man. His jet-black head of unkempt curls almost fell over his eyes.

'Pepa is Italian and an artist,' Sarah told Madge. 'He moved over here a few years ago. He has travelled the length and breadth of the country, painting all sorts of interesting landscapes.'

Sarah pulled out a large package wrapped up in brown paper to reveal a portrait of herself, which was a gift for her parents. Madge was very impressed. There was indeed an amazing likeness. Madge walked out of her sitting room.

'Bernard!' she called. 'Come and meet Sarah's young man!'

Sarah left for her parents then. Madge phoned Bronwyn straight away to fill her in.

'He's not a farmer, or a doctor, is he?' asked Bronwyn. 'Come on, Madge! Who is he?'

'More like, what is he?' said she to Bronwyn. 'He is far too good-looking for his own good! And he is one of these artist types living from hand to mouth.'

'Will he be able to provide for Sarah?' Bronwyn asked, more concerned than ever.

Sarah introduced Pepa to all her friends. She hugged her friend Tom. She was very glad that she had been able to help him and his wife after the loss of their first child.

'Well, Sarah, so you are finally ready to settle down?' said Tom. 'I thought you wouldn't go down that road for a long time. I'm delighted for you both. Will you move to Italy?'

'Not for a while,' said Sarah. 'Pepa is very happy here in Ireland. My mother and father like him and he likes them. They seem to have hit it off after he asked my father for my hand in marriage.'

'That will do it all right!' said Tom.

'So, all is well and that is the main thing, don't you think, Tom?' said Sarah, waiting for his approval. Tom nodded, but at the same time he worried for Sarah. She was like a sister to him and he wasn't at all sure about Pepa.

Tom had met many a charmer in his college years and Pepa was most certainly one of the same. Ellen and Emily were gobsmacked at Sarah getting such a catch. Tom made eye contact with Noel and he could see that he felt the same way about Pepa as he did. Why did Sarah have to have sand in her shoes? What was wrong with country life? She could have got a good man in her own country, an Irish chap, Tom thought.

Bronwyn arrived over at Tom and Ellen's house. She stood, almost reading his thoughts.

'Well, Tom?' she said, 'what do you think of her choice?'

'I only hope it is the right one,' he answered.

'I couldn't bear to see her with a broken heart,' said Bronwyn. 'She has grown into a beautiful young lady. Oh, I'm not so sure about him.'

'My sentiments exactly, Bronwyn,' said Tom.

The girls got talking amongst themselves after Sarah and Pepa left to visit some of her relatives.

'What do you think of him?' Ellen said first. 'I will wait and see but he seems a lovely person. But he is a good-looking man with buckets of charm. Will he have staying power in this relationship?'

'I think he might,' said Emily, 'they obviously love each other.'

'But for how long will Pepa stay faithful?' said Siobhan.

'Hold your horses, girls, and give him a chance! Let's just be happy for Sarah,' said Charlotte.

Meeting of Two Hearts

Sarah, Lucy and a few of her colleagues had gone to the large warehouse in Skeffington Street in Dublin to look at a selection of paintings. The girls always did something different one night a week, like a trip to the cinema, gallery or bowling. There was always plenty happening in the city. The warehouse is where Sarah first laid eyes on the most handsome man that she had ever seen. She mustered up the courage to say hello to him. She didn't want to seem rude as she walked slowly past. She would have to say something about his work if she wanted to get a good look at him. So, she took the bull by the horns, trying to sound confident, and said hello.

He returned her greeting in an Italian accent, an accent too die for.

'I almost did die, Em,' said Sarah, filling Emily and Siobhan in on how they had met.

He then spoke to her and somehow knew her name. She asked how he had known.

'Maybe I just guessed it,' he replied teasingly. 'You look like a Sarah! Only joking!' he said, and pointed to the name tag on her coat.

She had forgotten to take it off her cape when she came out of work. She hoped that she didn't look as stupid as she felt.

Lucy had whispered to Sarah, 'You two seem to be getting on well?'

'Why would he have an interest in me, Lucy?'

'Do you not see?' Lucy had answered. 'Have you looked in the mirror lately? You are a stunning girl with beautiful skin, lovely blond hair and a figure to die for. Don't underestimate yourself. He is the lucky one if he asks you out on a date! You both are like ebony and ivory,' she went on. 'You are so different. Think of the children you would have!'

They had both chuckled at the idea.

'Some chance of that!' Sarah had said. 'Slim to none, I'd say, given the fact we haven't even been on a date yet.'

Pepa did indeed ask Sarah out and they quickly became an item. They went everywhere together. No other woman would win Pepa's heart, though he could have had his pick of the finest of girls. When Sarah fell, she fell hard and she had never been love-struck before. Pepa had the largest brown eyes and longest eyelashes she had ever seen. His eyes were like black pools of water. He would mutter sweet nothings in her ear. It sounded so different in his language and it wouldn't have sounded nearly as seductive if he had come from Cork or Wexford, or any other county in Ireland for that matter.

Sarah had gazed into Pepa's eyes as he proposed to her.

'Are you sure, Pepa, that you are ready to settle down?'

'You are the one for me Sarah. The minute you walked through the door, I knew instantly.'

Sarah wanted to spend the rest of her life with this man and would travel the world with him. She hoped with all her heart he felt the same way about her. Sarah and Pepa had dated for a nearly a year and gotten on very well. They both had a great sense of humour. She could always see the funny side of things, even in the middle of chaos. Pepa knew that Sarah would never be a bore. He had left his philandering days behind him. She was everything he wanted in a woman and he hoped his parents would like her.

CHAPTER THIRTY-THREE

The Proposal

Raymond King decided that it was time to go back to see Siobhan. He had been in love with her for a very long time. He needed to finally know if she felt the same way about him. He hoped with all his heart his sense was right. If so, he would talk to her and see if they could get the right person to take over her fashion house. He had already been in touch with Emily and Noel, who he knew were very close to Siobhan. In fact, he knew that they were more like family.

Raymond arrived at their house on Tuesday evening at five o'clock. He was greeted by Emily, who brought him into the parlour for a cup of tea after his long journey. A bed had been made for Raymond in the spare room. All three sat down to tea after Emily had settled the children down for the night. Emily asked Raymond what his intentions were towards Siobhan. She just had to know. He had no hesitation in answering that he was in love with her and wanted to marry her and have a family. He told them that he couldn't get her out of his head.

'I just can't live without her,' he said. 'I hope with all my heart that she feels the same way about me.'

After tea Emily rang Siobhan and asked her to come over as she needed to discuss something important with her.

'Yes, no problem,' said Siobhan, 'just give me fifteen minutes. I'm just checking the last of the new stock.'

'Well, is it time to get the champagne glasses ready?' Noel whispered to his wife with a wink. Just in case, he had put a bottle in the fridge. Noel and Emily kept a bottle of the bubbly in case of a special occasion. They hoped this would be one and they would soon be celebrating Siobhan's very good fortune and Raymond getting the woman he loved.

Siobhan arrived wondering if everything was alright. She had put in a tiring day sorting out her new stock. She was very pleased at how the fashion house had taken off. A cup of tea was needed. Raymond was sitting at the table in the kitchen, and seemed very much at home. Emily led Siobhan's by the hand into the kitchen, saying, 'Come here quick I want your opinion on something, Siobhan.'

When Siobhan saw Raymond, shock took hold of her. She was at a loss for words. Raymond stood up from the chair and stepped towards her. Their eyes met.

'We meet again!' said Raymond. 'Will you spend some time with me over at the hotel? I need to talk to you Siobhan. I have taken much needed time off,' he continued. 'I know at last what I want. It has taken me a long time, but I'm ready to let go of my heavy workload. I have very good managers to look after the store for me. They'll probably do a better job. It's time now for me to make a life for myself. I want a family before it is too late.'

Then he got down on one knee and held out a beautiful diamond ring.

'I don't know how you feel about me, Siobhan. But one thing I am sure about is that I have loved you for a long time. I was hoping that you might feel the same way about me.'

Tears started to run down Siobhan's face. She couldn't believe what she was hearing. She thought she might have been dreaming.

Emily brought Siobhan a handkerchief to wipe away her tears. Finally, she blurted out the answer he was waiting for.

'Yes, Raymond, I feel the same way about you. But I always thought you would want to marry someone from the same background as yours, not a shop girl like me.'

'You are far from a shop girl, Siobhan. You have amazing talent and will be an asset to the store. You will be my wife, my confidant and the joint owner of my store. It will all be ours, Siobhan.'

Siobhan tried to take it all in. She couldn't quite believe it. Raymond gave her a gentle kiss. He too couldn't believe that he had got his heart's desire and was finally about to change his life for the better and he would no longer be a slave to the business anymore.

Noel and Emily could breathe easy now. Siobhan had been starving earlier now she didn't feel hungry at all! She could barely manage a cup of tea. The excitement was just too much to take in, even for Noel and Emily. Raymond and Siobhan had gotten what they both wanted at last.

Noel and Emily both went to the fridge at the same time and pulled out a bottle of ice-cold champagne.

'Gosh, Emily! I must make plans about what to do with the shop. Who will run it? And what will James and Jimmy think about it all! There's so much to think about!'

'Tomorrow is another day,' said Emily. 'Just enjoy tonight, Siobhan! We'll talk later.'

Raymond and Siobhan left for the hotel. Noel looked over at Emily. He was still in awe of her, and at that moment, he knew without a shadow of doubt that he would die without her in his life. He hoped that the same would happen for Siobhan and Raymond. He promptly gave her a long, lingering kiss, then said, 'The dishes can wait until morning don't you think, Em?'

Then they both went upstairs.

The following morning a list of people formed in Emily's head! She couldn't think straight she was so excited. It was all over the parish about Siobhan's engagement by then. Madge, Rose, Elizabeth and Bronwyn had heard, not to mention Beatrice. Everyone enjoyed Siobhan's very good fortune.

Siobhan asked Emily if she thought Beatrice might be interested in taking over the fashion house.

'She definitely would be the right person! She's a very wealthy woman who doesn't need the money but maybe could do with a hobby? What do you think, Em?'

Emily agreed saying, 'Everybody gets on well with her and she would keep the likes of Claire and her friends coming into the shop to buy those gorgeous clothes. Don't they look up to Beatrice, with her aristocratic background? She naturally just draws people together. I think it's something learned from being a politician's wife.'

The Challenge

When Beatrice was asked, she was shocked at first by the thought of the responsibility. But then she thought that of course she would manage. What on earth was she doing with her time anyway? It often seemed to her that she was filling in time. She would be still relatively young enough to take on such a task and a whole new life would open up for her.

Bronwyn and Rose called over to see Beatrice as to what she was going to do. They hoped for her sake that she would take over Siobhan's shop. They would offer to help her in whatever way they could and were already behaving like a couple of giddy schoolgirls.

Siobhan's solicitor would send all the documents to Beatrice's solicitor to make the arrangements for Beatrice to purchase the fashion house. The proceeds of the sale would go to Siobhan's brother, James, and their father, Jimmy. After all, Siobhan would be a very wealthy woman and wouldn't need the money from the sale.

Siobhan started to plan her wedding with the help of Bronwyn, Emily and her other close friends. She would rely on Bronwyn to stand in for her mother. Siobhan knew that is what her mother would have wished for. Bronwyn would be very happy to be an honorary mum for the day and during the lead up to the wedding. Emily, Ellen, Sarah and Charlotte were going to be her bridesmaids and matrons of honour. Siobhan spoke to Emily about what colour they should wear and what kind of material to go for. Emily suggested that the dresses should be pure silk. They should be burnt orange for an August wedding, almost Autumn.

'The flowers must be orange and cream roses then,' said Siobhan. 'On the altar, I'd like lilies as they were Mammy's favourite flower. It would be a fitting tribute to her to have them on the altar. And they'll remind Daddy of his wedding day,' she said with tears in her eyes.

'How could you forget your mother! Sure, that wouldn't be possible at all, Siobhan!' said Bronwyn as she gave Siobhan a motherly hug.

Bronwyn bought a deep purple dress and matching wool jacket, with black patent shoes and a small bag to match. As she looked in the mirror at her outfit, she thought to herself with a chuckle, I still have it! Madge couldn't decide between a yellow dress with a large collar and mid-length sleeves or a simple cream dress with short sleeves and matching jacket. Mary encouraged her saying, 'Madge, this isn't the time not to play it safe. The cream is nice, but the yellow is fabulous on you!'

All the others agreed with Mary. Even Bernard threw in his tuppence worth, saying, 'You are a sight to behold, Madge!'

Mary then shooed him out of the busy sitting room.

When Bronwyn made the bookings at the local hotel, she reminded them that everything would have to be perfect for all Mr King's family and his special guests for the duration of their stay.

'Everything must be just right from the minute they walk through the door,' Bronwyn said. 'There are to be no half measures and there must be only the finest of everything, from crockery to silverware. I hope the new carpet in the entrance will be ready. Then the main ballroom can be turned into a dining room for the wedding party. Don't forget the bedrooms and bathrooms must be spotless for Siobhan and Raymond and all their guests from the United Kingdom,' she said. 'Mr King has asked me to let you know that he will help out with the costs for the refurbishment of the hotel. You'll be getting quite a bit of money, which won't be an issue for him. He just wants to have everything in place for his family and friends. Siobhan's wish is to get married in her hometown.' She went on, 'it'll bring much needed business to the parish as well and for that we all should be very thankful. And let us be proud of our parish and everything it has to offer, with everyone giving it their all. At least one hundred people will be over from England, not counting half the parish invited by Siobhan's father and her brother. As you know, James is a first-time candidate in the local elections and is very popular in the parish. It'll be the wedding of the year, or maybe even of the century in Kilton,' finished a very excited Bronwyn.

The Excitement of It All

The day started off wet. Bronwyn couldn't believe it. She had put out a statue of the Child of Prague to keep away the rain, praying out loud to her favourite saint. She thought that it would be awful if all the visitors from England were to leave with the memory of a wet, miserable day and prayed to the lady in blue that she might have a change of heart for all their sakes.

Madge came to help Bronwyn. She had fallen in a large pothole and was covered in muck from head to toe. Oliver had heard Madge's cry for help.

He rushed to her and helped her up, at the same time as she was trying to wipe herself down.

'Don't worry about me,' said Madge, 'Thank God I'm not dressed for the wedding yet! But for God's sake, Oliver! Get someone over to sort out this pothole. We can't have anyone else fall into it.'

Oliver was as excited as everybody else in the parish. News had travelled far and wide. There was going to be an influx of people arriving by buses just to get a look at the bride and groom. Some of the locals believed that anyone who lived across the water were different from the Irish people. As far as they were concerned they were foreigners.

Oliver had a spring in his step. It didn't matter to him that it had been raining all night, but now it looked like it would be a better day. He made his way around the village, mustering up any help he could get with pouring gravel in the potholes. He went about his task whistling and thinking that he might meet a nice foreign woman himself and how he scrubbed up well in his navy suit, white shirt and new black shoes. He hadn't minded spending the few bob, as it was an investment in himself. He wanted to give the impression that he was a person of some means, a person who stood out.

He walked out his front door, which he seldom used. He considered how today was a special day. He was an important guest and that was something to be reckoned with. He had spent half the day yesterday washing and polishing his black Austin, right down to the wheels. He looked in the car mirror and said to himself, 'You're a fine-looking man. Aren't all the women mad about me! But it's bachelorhood for me, for now at least.'

He hopped into his car, singing 'Blue Suede Shoes,' full of a great anticipation of what the day might bring.

CHAPTER THIRTY-FOUR

An Easter Blessing

Emily was in labour with their fourth, an Easter baby. She had said that there was no need to ring Bronwyn and that she was ready to go. Noel had the farm taken care of and it was time to ring his mother to come to mind the children. Emily's parents had been waiting for the phone call and had everything ready, so it would only take them a couple of minutes to reach the house. Emily sat while her housekeeper made her a cup of tea and told her to get it down and not to worry about anything.

The children were very excited at the thought of a new baby in the house. The twins kept asking about their grandfather, Howard, and why he wouldn't come and visit them. They asked if he didn't like them because they were bold.

'Hush now, children,' Emily would say, 'don't you know that granddad Howard is not well!'

It would be their last, as she and Noel felt four children was enough. Emily was hoping it would be a boy this time and that they would be having a blue christening cake.

At three thirty on a Tuesday afternoon, the twenty-fifth of April, Noel John Howard Junior was born into the Howard household. A large bunch of yellow roses arrived at the hospital for Mrs Emily Howard.

'My goodness!' exclaimed Emily. 'We won't be able to fit anymore flowers into the room.'

'Ah, I think you'll fit this special bunch of roses, Em!'

Noel handed the flowers to the nurse. They were from Siobhan and Raymond. There was a letter attached from Siobhan.

I will be over on an Aer Lingus flight in three weeks' time. James will pick me up from the airport and I will be staying with daddy but I will be spending my time over with you Em, giving you a hand. I have some important news of my own. It is not out yet Em but myself and Raymond are expecting our first child. I just couldn't hold it in. I just had to tell you both. I can't wait to see you and your beautiful baby boy and of course the rest of the gang. Love from your very best friend,
Siobhan

A Time of Peace

Bernard and Madge stood outside their shop on a warm summer night, enjoying the peace and quiet after a long day's work. The stream that ran through the village glistened in the moonlight. The row of trees on either side stood like soldiers, as if they were on guard and all was well with the world. All was well with Madge and Bernard.

Bronwyn for once took a few days off. She found it hard to leave her work behind as there was always someone who needed her and wouldn't be happy with anyone else. But this time they would just will have to get used to her not being there. She explained to her friends that she was going to Paris for four days to see her friend Joseph.

'Of course, you know we were once the best of friends, Madge?' she said with a dreamy expression, thinking of times gone by. 'In my heart, I will always have a special place for him.'

The Heart of a Schoolgirl Once Again

'But now, Madge,' Bronwyn said with girlish excitement, 'I'm looking forward to meeting all of Joseph's friends, and of course seeing the sites of Paris! Joseph has booked me into a fancy hotel not far his apartment. God, Madge! I just can't wait!' She knew for certain her friend would have booked an evening at the opera.

'What will I wear?' Bronwyn continued. 'I think it's time to go to Beatrice. She won't let me down. She will help me to pick out an evening dress for the occasion, and maybe help me pack.'

CHAPTER THIRTY-FIVE

A Time of Great Confusion!

Madge had asked for Emily's help with Mary's upcoming wedding to Myles O'Riordan. Madge said of him that, 'he's a nice enough chap but not one of our own.' But any boy would come under the same scrutiny and Emily wondered who would she count as one of them? Someone who lived in the parish and came from a business background? But Mary had other ideas of what she wanted in a young man.

She had met Myles in the bowling alley in Wicklow. Bowling was a favourite pastime of hers and her friends' Rebecca and Molly. Mary and Myles had hit it off straight away. After the bowling, the girls and boys had made their way over to Harvey's Diner for a coke. Mary had felt very much that they were at ease with Myles.

Mary got to know all about his life. He too had lost his father young and it had put a stop to him going to secondary school, as he had had to help his mother to bring in much-needed money. He had had no choice in the matter of his education at all. Mary was sorry for him and felt drawn to him even more. Myles couldn't believe his luck, with a good-looking girl like Mary taking such an interest in him, a person of no standing whatsoever. He couldn't get enough of Mary, and she felt very protective towards him.

Mary sometimes felt smothered by her two guardians. At the same time, she was very glad that they cared for her so much. She often wondered what would have happened to her without them? She tried to imagine her life without Bernard and Madge and a shiver would run down her spin.

Mary spoke to Emily and Charlotte about the situation and how she felt torn between Myles and her parents. She wondered how she could convince them that he was the right person for her. Madge wanted the best possible life for her and worried about what would he could have to offer, being a farmhand with nothing of his own.

Mary pulled out her little box of trinkets, taking out her gold chain and locket. She held it close to her heart and wondered what her parents would have thought of Miles. Would they have approved of her choice?

Eventually she told Madge and Bernard then that it didn't matter what they thought of him.

'Like it or not, I'm going to marry him, Mammy,' she said.

'If you are sure that he is the one for you, love, then we won't stand in your way. But Mary,' Madge went on, 'you are used to such a nice life. Will Myles provide that for you? There is only so much that you can bring to the table as a bank clerk. How will you manage when children come along? As far as I can see you are letting yourself in for a life of hardship. It will be a big struggle if you marry him.'

Madge pleaded with tears in her eyes.

Mary knew that Madge and Bernard were right. She wondered if it was too late to call off the wedding. The invitations had not gone out yet. Madge had had her wedding dress altered to fit Mary. She had been very happy that Mary had chosen to wear her wedding dress but still had her concerns.

'I only hope Myles is the right man for her,' Madge said to Bernard. 'Maybe he will be a good provider by some miracle. I just can't see how that will happen.'

Madge thought back then to all those years when she thought she would never have someone to pass her dress onto and how all that mattered was that she was so glad that she had a lovely girl like Mary to look after and that she just wanted her to be happy.

Mary was very quiet at dinner. Madge tried talking about the floral arrangements for the church. Mary burst into tears.

'Mammy, what am I going to do?' she cried. 'I can't marry Myles! I know now that I just felt sorry for him and that deep-down I don't love him at all. It was more like caring for a friend.'

Bernard rose and went over to Mary.

'Don't worry, love, I will go with you when you tell Myles. We will let him down gently. Sooner or later Myles would have realised getting married was a bad idea.'

At that moment, Mary just wanted to run up to her bedroom and never come out. Mary felt like she hadn't the strength to face up to this awful situation.

Bernard drove over to ask Myles to call over after tea as there was something they wanted to discuss. Myles arrived at the shop later wondering what this was about. He hoped what money he had saved would be enough for the wedding. There was no one he could borrow from. Perspiration started to form on his forehead. He waited for Mary to speak and wasn't at all prepared for what he was about to hear. He started to cry.

'Oh, Mary! I love you so much. But in my heart, I knew you didn't feel the same way about me. I had hoped that in time you would come to love me. You were so good to me and treated me like I was someone, and I will be forever grateful to you. How am I going to live without you?'

'I'll always be there for you' said Mary. 'And in time you'll meet the right woman and you will be glad that we didn't marry.'

They were both crying and Madge also shed tears for this young man, and for her kind-hearted daughter.

On Sunday morning, Bernard and Madge asked Mary if she and Rebecca would like to go over to Wicklow for afternoon tea.

'Just like the old days,' said Bernard.

'Yes, just like the old days, Daddy,' answered Mary and gave him a big hug.

CHAPTER THIRTY-SIX

Paris, Here I Come!

Beatrice was delighted for her friend Bronwyn. She hadn't seen anyone looking so forward to a holiday in a long time. Bronwyn was like a giddy schoolgirl. They set about the important task of dressing Bronwyn for her trip, but were soon interrupted by a gentle rap on the door. John was standing outside.

'I'll collect you at seven thirty if that is alright with you, Beatrice?' he said.

'Perfect, John. Looking forward to a nice dinner,' she said.

Bronwyn looked at both of them in wonder at such a match.

'Well, Beatrice. You are a dark horse,' she said when John was gone. 'Are you and John an item, then? How long is this going on? I thought I knew just about everything that went on here in Kilton!'

'My car broke down just outside Kilton,' said Beatrice. 'I was on the way back from Dublin about five miles down the road, when John and Elizabeth's husband, Paddy, arrived on the scene.

The Awakening

'They gave me a lift home,' Beatrice continued, 'and John arranged for Collier's Garage to collect the car and sort it out for me. He then offered me a lift to wherever I needed to go. We got on well. He's a real gentleman. I thought that I would never have feelings for anyone except Freddy. I wasn't at all prepared for what has happened to me. We are so different yet so at ease with each other. I have been over on his farm and I love all the animals. John bought me my first pair of wellingtons,' Beatrice laughed. 'I was a sight for sore eyes, even if I do say so myself. I just loved every minute of it! What do you think, Bronwyn?'

Bronwyn could hardly breath with impatience to tell Madge and to get her opinion on this new development. Just then, Bronwyn herself got a pang in her heart. She wondered if she and Andrew would make a go of it. They had been keeping each other company for quite a while now. All she had to do was say yes and he would have her up at the altar in jig time.

What is the Meaning of Freedom?

It was now or never. But could she give up her freedom? Bronwyn was so set in her ways. But all the same she thought how it would be lovely to have someone sitting by the fire with her of an evening, chatting about their day. A warm feeling washed over her. Was it embarrassment at the thought of sex? Never having had experience, she worried if she would cope, and then it would be too late after they married. She needed to have a serious talk with Andrew. Maybe they just might get together in Dublin on a weekend away? But she knew this simply was not done. She could hardly believe she was thinking such things. But these were life changing decisions. If all went well, then marriage would be on the horizon. If not, then neither of them would speak of it again. Bronwyn felt embarrassed thinking about sex outside marriage. But was it really a mortal sin? Who said so? The Pope over in Rome? But he was a mere man. Maybe he shouldn't be taken so seriously? After all, what would he really know about such things?

Bronwyn decided she would go to confession in Dublin where her voice wouldn't be recognised. If Andrew and herself were to marry, then there wouldn't be any repenting to be done, only a good life ahead for the both.

Bronwyn asked Andrew to bring her to the airport. On her return, they could stay in Dublin for a night or two and no one would be any the wiser. Both were delighted with the arrangement. In the meantime, she thought, Paris here I come! It would be the perfect place to buy satin lingerie and her favourite Chanel perfume. Bronwyn was almost overwhelmed by what was happening in her life. She had resigned herself to being alone but maybe this was her time. Looking up at the heavens she wondered if God had totally forgotten her?

All the Friends Together Once Again

Emily, Ellen and Charlotte had organised a get-together for Siobhan. She was coming over to Emily's house for a couple of weeks with her twin boys, six months old already, and 'a handful', she would say to Madge and Bronwyn with sheer delight. She would have more comfort staying with Emily. All the girls rallied around for their friend Siobhan. Emily was good at giving the orders and getting everything ready for this surprise party.

Madge and Bronwyn were right in the middle of it all, and why wouldn't they be, since they had known Siobhan since a young girl and was very much part of her life. They would have to cater for the party at the local hotel, with all their children there. It would make much more sense with all the families and their many friends. Bronwyn explained to Rose,

'You understand that the party will have be in the hotel with all the babies down on the floor?'

Of course, she understood that they couldn't do it in a smoky pub full of farmers. Even the use of the room that held Macra na Feirme meetings wouldn't do for the babies with the smell of cigarettes.

'What about me lending a hand?' said Rose.

'All hands-on deck would be most welcome and don't forget to ask Elizabeth too, just in case she feels left out, Rose? It will be great to get the chance to spend time together to catch up. The more the merrier!'

They hung up balloons, streamers and a big poster with the babies' names on it. The ballroom was also festooned with blue decorations. Everyone was catered for with cold and hot platters, and Alice Lyons supplied a huge cake with blue and white icing, with the boys' names on top. The babies had been named Brian James after Siobhan's mother's father, Jimmy, and Raymond Louis after Raymond's father.

'Where are the fresh cream cakes, Emily?' asked Bronwyn.

'Charlotte is on the way over with them,' answered Emily, and Bronwyn sighed with relief.

Charlotte bustled into the room laden with bags, with Sarah marching behind her with as many bags again.

'Did you think you could hold this party without me?' she said to Emily. Both girls embraced each other.

'Where is Pepa?' asked Emily, noticing Sarah wasn't wearing her ring.

'Not with me this time. I'm taking a break as I'm not so sure I want to be that adventurous. Oh, I always said I needed to get away from here, but you know Em, I am not so sure anymore. I miss everyone, my family and Bronwyn, Madge and all of you my friends. I just want to enjoy my time off from work this weekend. I'm so looking forward to catching up with Siobhan, her babies and everyone else. It's very hard work in the hospital,' she continued, 'but you know I'm not afraid of hard work. Even though the hospital is busy all the time, it can be lonely at times. Though I've made some nice friends up in Dublin. I thought that was what I wanted but I'm not so sure anymore. I guess you could say I am at a crossroads in my life. But I think I want to come back home. But mums the word for the moment!'

CHAPTER THIRTY-SEVEN

The Surprise Party

The guests were on their way to the party. Noel gave Emily and Siobhan a helping hand with carrying in the little ones. Charlotte brought Siobhan to the hotel thinking they were having afternoon tea with the girls. They were barely up the steps, when they heard a great roar.

'Surprise!'

Siobhan started to cry overwhelmed by what they had done for her. She cried and laughed at the same time, seeing all her friends and her mentors, Bronwyn and Madge. She told them that she loved them both and gave each of them a kiss on the cheek.

'Mammy would be so thankful to all of you,' she said, 'for looking after her when she couldn't. She died far too young.'

Noel was called out to the reception of the hotel. His mother needed to speak to him. She asked her son if he hated his father.

'No, Mum,' he said. 'I have made a life without my father. I was heartbroken for a very long time. Each occasion was marred by his absence. Many is the time I wanted to ask his advice on something and then it would hit me that he wasn't there anymore. It was like he died a long time ago. Now I have a good life with Emily and my four children, and, of course, you, Mum. I don't know what I would have done without you, if you had deserted me too. I have a very good relationship with my father-in-law and he has been very good to me altogether. I still love my father and am just sad that he is missing out on his beautiful grandchildren and a lovely woman like Emily.'

'Maybe it's time to end all this, would you agree, Noel? Will you come over to the house for tea with Emily and the children?'

'Well, I won't have him treating Emily and our children badly and ignoring them. I have so much respect for my wife that I won't let that happen.'

'Don't worry son, it is time,' said his tearful mother.

Beatrice arrived with John. Both appeared very happy in each other's company. They were a good match. All their friends were very happy for them. Andrew went over to Bronwyn and kissed her on the cheek.

'Bronwyn, would this be a good time to announce our engagement?' he asked.

'I think it would be a perfect time and setting, and Siobhan won't mind one bit, with us taking some of the limelight off her for a few minutes.'

Bronwyn was totally in love with Andrew and life just got better and better. She was very happy, so a short engagement was just the ticket. Bronwyn couldn't wait to walk down the aisle with Madge as her matron of honour. Maybe Beatrice and John would follow them down the aisle too, she thought, soon?

'Emily, I know you had your party quite a while ago,' said Alice, 'but I have baked you a christening cake for your little boy and this is the perfect occasion for it. Sure, you and Siobhan couldn't be separated as youngsters. I have watched you stay close friends as young adults and now you two are more like sisters. So, this is an important occasion for you both.'

Alice gave Emily a hug.

Charlotte, Ellen and Sarah were hugging each other, tears rolling down their cheeks.

'Come on!' shouted Oliver. 'Is this a wake or a party?'

He busied himself going around to everyone making sure that they had enough tea and coffee, and plenty of cake. 'And not a woman in sight?' he sighed.

Madge laughed at his matter-of-fact way.

'Maybe that's why he is free and single!' she said to Bronwyn. 'The confirmed bachelor for now, until some woman pulls at his heartstrings and that will be the end of his wandering and having a good time, don't you think?'

Bernard and Madge had taken a half day and brought Mary along to the party. It wasn't all about work. This was a day to be celebrated. Bernard admired Madge's green dress.

'You look lovely, love. I suppose I should tell you more often. Don't you agree, Mary, that she's a fine woman? And where would the both of us be without her?' he said, giving Madge a hug.

Mary loved her new parents and knew she owed them a huge debt of gratitude. But Madge and Bernard's lives had changed for the better when Mary and her father had entered them.

A Change of Heart

Noel told Emily that he had to make a stop over at his parent's farm for a couple of minutes. The children were delighted at the chance to see their grandmother. Noel pulled into the yard and his mother came out the back door, drying her hands on her apron. Noel's father made his way towards his son. His eyes were full of tears. He apologised to him for his arrogance, for cutting him off from the family and for all the heartbreak he had caused Noel.

'Your poor mother has aged years over me being so pig-headed. I love you son, with all my heart, and I'm so sorry for all those missed years! Do you think Emily and yourself can see a way of forgiving me and coming back into my life?'

Emily jumped out of the jeep, ran to Noel's mother and his father, and kissed them both.

'I love your family with all my heart,' she told Noel's father. 'Your grand-children always believed you weren't well. That is why they couldn't come to visit, so there is no dislike for you in their little hearts.'

At that moment Bronagh lifted the baby out of the jeep. The twins hopped out and ran to their grandparents, hugging them both. The baby did not want to be left out and made his presence known. Noel's father couldn't get enough of the children.

'Imagine these four are our very own grandchildren,' he said. 'Isn't it great altogether, Noel?'

Then they all sat down to tea and warm apple pie.

Arrangements had to be made for the family to move into the farmhouse. Painting was done in the bedrooms and everything looked a lot brighter in the house. Bronagh and the younger ones and couldn't be kept indoors, always out with their grandfather. Emily's family were thrilled with this change of heart when both families got together to make up for lost time.

Noel stood in awe of his beautiful wife. She looked stunning, even after giving birth to four children, He was very proud of Emily and had no problem in telling her so.

'It's about time for a break away, Emily,' he said. 'Both sets of parents agree we need a few days off. We are both exhausted. What do you think of Kerry? The scenery is lovely down there. God, Emily!' he went on. 'I feel the same way about you now as when I first laid eyes on you that first time at the dance. What do you say? You and me, on our own just for four or five days with plenty of room service?'

He gave her that cheeky wink of his. Emily kissed him, not caring what anyone thought. All that mattered at that moment was the two of them being together and the family being back together again.